PRAISE FOR *Serenade for Nadia*

"Compelling...fearless and eloquent."

—*Wall Street Journal*

"[An] affecting novel about love, loss, and personal identity...Livaneli smoothly switches between 2001 and
1938–1942, offering insights into Turkey's rich cultural,
political, ethnic, and religious divides. Livaneli's worthy
portrait of a man coming to terms with his tragic past
and a woman coming to terms with her Turkish heritage
delivers a forceful plea for openness and tolerance."

—*Publishers Weekly*

"Heartbreakingly vivid...Livaneli's passion in exposing
Turkey's and the West's culpability in real massacres is
eloquent... [*Serenade for Nadia* is] hard to forget."

—*Kirkus Reviews*

"Writer. Musician. Philosopher. Zülfü Livaneli is one of my favorite authors. With *Serenade for Nadia*, he has written a masterpiece about love and music, connecting Turkey's complex and rich history to the present day. So happy that Livaneli's words can now inspire millions more with this new English translation, and that the world will get to know one of the true cultural treasures coming out of Turkey."

—Hamdi Ulukaya, CEO of Chobani

"This wonderfully evocative novel does far more than introduce one of Turkey's great creative artists to American audiences. It is also a fast-paced and intensely emotional account of modern history that leads us to reflect on the ways that people and nations confront their past."

—Stephen Kinzer, author of *Crescent and Star: Turkey Between Two Worlds*

PRAISE FOR *Disquiet*

"Entirely captivating." —*New York Times Book Review*

"[An] arresting novel." —*The New Yorker*

"A tale of identities colliding from a writer who's held five passports... [*Disquiet*] unfolds in a border town caught between its ancient past and tumultuous present."

—NPR, *All Things Considered*

"A somber, pensive novel, by one of Turkey's greatest modern writers... Livaneli's slender narrative contains multitudes... [An] intensely emotional, memorable story."

—*Kirkus Reviews* (starred review)

"A keenly wrought story... [whose] urgency comes through in its tight grasp on the problems of religious violence, misogyny, and the failures of compassion. The result is a memorable illumination of the Yezidi people's rich history."

—*Publishers Weekly*

"A penetrating novel... indelible fiction based on real-life horror... [*Disquiet*] will demand attention, provoke outrage, perhaps even inspire lifesaving change."

—*Shelf Awareness*

"A moving novel set entirely in the modern-day Middle East." —*PopSugar*, Best New Books of the Month

"Impactful... [a] fascinating novel about a man caught between cultures."   —*Foreword Reviews*

PRAISE FOR *The Last Island*

"This haunting fable of a President's war against seagulls feels all the more relevant to our times in its absurdity and heartbreak. Livaneli has written a lucid account of a community's shattering alongside natural devastation. A wise and piercing book."

—Ayşegül Savaş, author of *White on White* and *Walking on the Ceiling*

"In this beautifully written book, Livaneli poetically recounts the story of how societies get corrupted by self-serving autocratic leaders. Livaneli's riveting *The Last Island* provides a much-needed and uplifting read for all in need of resilience and hope."

—Soner Cagaptay, author of *A Sultan in Autumn: Erdogan Faces Turkey's Uncontainable Forces*

"With this novel Livaneli has entered through the grand gates of literature."

—Yashar Kemal, author of *Memed, My Hawk*

"Urgent and allegorical, Livaneli is masterful in his depiction of how authoritarian power destroys a community's people and environment. *The Last Island* is a stunning novel that will stay with me for a long time."

—Mina Seçkin, author of *The Four Humors*

"This book is a recipe of what authoritarianism is made of. Some readers might start the reading thinking this is only directed to current politics in Turkey. However, it quickly emerges that it is about decades of power struggles, with a message that within this vicious circle there are no happy endings."

—Louis Fishman, author of *Jews and Palestinians in the Late Ottoman Era, 1908–1914: Claiming the Homeland*

"Human nature and authority come face-to-face in Livaneli's unparalleled, creative novel. The author invites us to rethink the world we live in."

—Lenore Martin, Emmanuel College and Harvard University

The Fisherman and His Son

ALSO BY ZÜLFÜ LIVANELI

The Last Island

Disquiet

Serenade for Nadia

Bliss

The
Fisherman
and
His Son

ZÜLFÜ LIVANELI

Translated from the Turkish by Brendan Freely

OTHER PRESS
NEW YORK

Production editor: Yvonne E. Cárdenas
Text designer: Jennifer Daddio / Bookmark Design & Media Inc.
This book was set in Baskerville and Baka Too
by Alpha Design & Composition of Pittsfield, NH

1 3 5 7 9 10 8 6 4 2

Library of Congress Cataloging-in-Publication Data
Names: Livaneli, Zülfü, 1946- author. | Freely, Brendan, 1959- translator.
Title: The fisherman and his son / Zülfü Livaneli ; translated from the
Turkish by Brendan Freely.
Other titles: Balıkçı ve oğlu. English
Description: New York : Other Press, [2022]
Identifiers: LCCN 2022050271 (print) | LCCN 2022050272 (ebook) |
ISBN 9781635423662 (paperback) | ISBN 9781635423679 (ebook)
Subjects: LCGFT: Domestic fiction. | Novels.
Classification: LCC PL248.L58 B3513 2022 (print) |
LCC PL248.L58 (ebook) | DDC 894/.3533—dc23/eng/20221221
LC record available at https://lccn.loc.gov/2022050271
LC ebook record available at https://lccn.loc.gov/2022050272

Perhaps I should not have been
a fisherman, he thought.
But that was the thing that I was born for.

ERNEST HEMINGWAY, *The Old Man and the Sea*

A PASSION FOR HEMINGWAY

I'm sure I had toys when I was a child, but I don't remember any of them. I suppose I didn't have much interest in toys. However, when I was in primary school in the ancient city of Amasya, where my father was serving as prosecutor, I subscribed to three magazines: *Children's Nest, Pecos Bill,* and *Köroğlu.* It gave me such a nice feeling to have these three magazines delivered to the house in my name. I would bury myself in the pages of the magazines, spending hours in what for me was a sea of pleasure. My head would spin from the savor of those magazines. I was also a fan of the adventures of Sadık Demir in a comic strip in the newspaper that was delivered to our house every day. I later learned that this was a translation of the American comic strip *Oaky Doaks,* by R. B. Fuller.

Years later, when I was in middle school in Ankara, my passion for books became excessive. I read whatever I could get my hands on, but I was particularly taken by the American novelists Ernest Hemingway, Jack London, Erskine Caldwell, and John Steinbeck. (When I was a little older they would be joined by William Faulkner.) The walls of my bedroom were covered with pictures of Hemingway. Every Saturday I would go to the American library, secretly cut out articles about Hemingway from magazines like *Life*, bring them home, and file them. On my desk there were copies of Hemingway's novels in the original English and in Turkish translation. I read every line of every biography written about him, including the one by his brother, Leicester. Hemingway gave me a sense of freedom. I wanted to live the endless future before me as he had lived. I knew deep down that I was not going to live an ordinary life like everyone else. My passion for Hemingway led me to some crazy experiences. But first I have to talk about the secret temple of books I created in my room.

At first my parents were pleased that I read so much, but later, when it got out of control, it began to bother them. I even remember my mother tearing up one of my books. I was doing badly in school; I couldn't get up in the morning. What I considered my real life took place at night, when I was alone with my books. Most of my friends would go to the coffeehouse to play cards or backgammon. I'd never even been to a coffeehouse, and I never learned to play backgammon, pool, or cards.

In the end my father had to forbid me to read books. Every night, after everyone had gone to bed, he would come to check if any light was streaming through the frosted-glass panel in my door. If he saw light, he would immediately come in and tell me to go to sleep—if not, he would walk away quietly. For several nights I was unable to read, I just tossed and turned in bed. Then I found a solution. I realized that I could fit under the bed, and that the bedcovers reached to the floor; if I tucked them in carefully, I would be completely concealed. I spread a blanket on the stone floor. And the little lamp I plugged in provided plenty of light. I checked several times from outside, and no light leaked out. From then on I enjoyed my nights immensely. I brought in a pile of books and a plate of fruit, and explored paradise until morning. When either of my parents passed the door, they thought I'd finally got over reading too much and that I was sound asleep.

The intensive reading I did at such a young age brought benefits. When I did an adaption for radio of Hemingway's *For Whom the Bell Tolls* it was of great help in learning to write dialogue. When the *Milliyet* newspaper held a writing contest, I visited several juvenile detention centers and wrote a piece called "Child Of-fenders." Under Hemingway's influence, I wrote a novel about the life of a bullfighter named Amarillo. I'm sure it was terrible, but as a cocky fifteen-year-old I'd written my first book.

I'd had a cyst behind my ear for as long as I could remember. It pushed my ear forward and was visible in all my childhood photographs. They gave me no anesthesia, and it took them fifty minutes to scrape out the cyst. Because it was so close to my ear, the scraping sound was unnervingly loud. As if the operation was being broadcast over speakers. But I was completely at ease, because two days earlier I'd read about how the knight Pardaillan hadn't flinched when he received a sword wound. But Hemingway was my real inspira-tion. If he had withstood so much pain, I was going to bear this in silence. After the operation, the doctor looked at me in amazement and said, "Bravo, what a brave boy you are!" He had no idea that books could serve as an anesthetic.

I read all of Hemingway's books many times, but *The Old Man and the Sea*, which I knew almost by heart, had a special place for me. I felt as if I knew Santiago, who was "*salao*, which is the worst form of unlucky." I could feel the salt of the Caribbean on my skin. I could taste the sour flavor of herring.

Preface

When I saw the Caribbean for the first time at the age of forty-four, I felt as if I knew it, as if it had been part of my childhood.

There was a vast difference between the enchanting world of Hemingway and my monotonous life in Ankara. I moved back and forth between my house and my school, and life seemed dull and meaningless. School was incredibly boring.

INTRODUCING HEMINGWAY
TO HANNIBAL

As the end of the school year approaches, the weight of bad grades and boredom becomes like a mountain sitting on your chest. Depressed and discouraged, there's nothing to do but simply wait for summer to begin. The monotonous and depressing days follow each other relentlessly, and you don't know what to do.

The smell of spring in the air stirs the blood. Youthful nights are marked by the heady scent of the acacia trees. Nature is in ferment, seeds are sprouting and sap is flowing, and all you can do is sit in your room reading a book and watching flies come in through the window. And if, like me, you've failed seven subjects, life seems like a ball of interwoven problems from which you can never extricate yourself.

When I got my report card and saw just how bad it was, I did something I'd never done before: I went to a soccer game. I don't know if this was a reaction or if I was trying to escape. Ankaragücü was playing a team called Amerigo. The foreign team toyed with Ankaragücü like a cat playing with a mouse. The final score was 7-0.

When I encountered the unfortunate number seven again, it seemed more than a coincidence. I went home and got a couple of books and some other things. I put what little money I'd saved from my allowance in my pocket and left the house. It was almost dark when I reached the bus terminal. I was able to find a seat at the very back of the Istanbul bus. A friend of mine had told me good things about two coastal towns called Eskihisar and Darıca. Especially after *The Old Man and the Sea*, I could think of nothing but fishing, the sea, and adventure.

Toward morning I got off the bus at a gas station on the Ankara-Istanbul highway. It was dark; all I could see was the gas station and two roadside coffeehouses. I went into one of them and drank tea with the bus drivers and passengers. I asked the waiter, who was about my age, about Eskihisar. He pointed behind the coffeehouse and said there was a road down to the sea through the woods. It was five kilometers.

"The forest wardens will be here soon," he said. "I'll send you down with them."

The forest wardens arrived just as dawn was breaking, and we set off after they'd finished their tea. We descended though a dense, healthy pine forest. I answered their questions by telling them I was a student who wanted to go camping. I wasn't going to tell them I'd confused myself by reading too many books.

After a difficult trek, we reached the small fishing village of Eskihisar ("old castle") near Hannibal's tomb. Thousands of years ago this had been Libyssa in the kingdom of Bithynia. I'd read that the Carthaginian general Hannibal committed suicide here, and had been buried here according to his wishes. I sat by his tomb and read *The Old Man and the Sea* aloud. I felt as if I was introducing Hannibal and Hemingway. Eskihisar reminded me of that fishing village in the Caribbean. I felt as if I'd entered Hemingway's novel, as if I'd found the place I would live for the rest of my life.

There was a nice coffeehouse under the large plane tree at the entrance to the village. It was run by a man named Hasan. I told him I was a student from Ankara on vacation. The ancient Anatolian tradition of helping strangers, a tradition that would save my life many times over the years, was immediately put into practice. Everyone tried to help me because I was a guest from God. Hasan put out the word, then told me

I could stay with an old woman who lived on the hill. He pointed to her house. It was apart from the other houses of the village, a dilapidated wooden house standing alone at the top of the hill.

I immediately went down to the beach, found a secluded spot, and read Hemingway until evening, enjoying the sea and my freedom. In the evening I ate fresh fried fish at Hasan's place. My back and shoulders were sunburned but I felt good.

It was late when I set out for the house where I was going to stay. I started climbing the hill. I passed the edge of the village. As I walked by moonlight toward the spooky-looking house, I suddenly found myself in a graveyard. I felt as if I'd moved from an adventure movie to a horror movie. I had goosebumps by the time I reached the wooden house. The door was open and I went in. There wasn't a sound to be heard. The floorboards creaked under my feet as I called out to ask if anyone was home. I heard a moan from the back of the house and moved in that direction. I entered a room, and in the moonlight streaming in through the window I saw a strange-looking old woman, who I later learned was bedridden. She looked at me without saying anything, occasionally letting out a moan. I went up to the top floor, lay on the first bed I found, and slept an uneasy sleep punctuated by nightmares.

I left the house at first light and told Hasan I wasn't going to be able to stay in that house. I also said that I wanted to work, and to learn about fishing. Hasan spoke to a fisherman and found me a job. I was going to work for a man known as Sergeant. I would gather nets, clean the boat, and help with the fishing. I began work eagerly, and later Sergeant told me I could sleep in the boat.

We set out early in the morning to pull up nets and longlines. Sergeant taught me how to find schools of fish, how to cast the nets and pull them up, and showed me sea creatures I'd never seen before. Sometimes he showed me how to use a spear gun.

He always stood over me as he taught me to put the nets that could still be used in the boat and toss those that could no longer be used into the sea. Once I found a strange, gray creature in the net; it looked a bit like a turbot. There didn't seem to be any place to take hold of it; all I could see was a single hole. I was just reaching for it when Sergeant hurriedly grabbed my hand. If I put my finger in that hole, the fish would tear my hand off.

I slept in the boat in the open air, watching the stars and enjoying my salty adventure. I decided to spend the rest of my life in Eskihisar, fishing and writing books. I didn't want any other kind of life.

The only thing that bothered me was how unfair I'd been to my family. At that age I was so fond of adventure I wasn't too aware of this unfairness, yet it still bothered me, and slowly I began to be tortured by feelings of guilt.

Two months later I decided to go to Ankara, talk to my family, and tell them everything. (Later I was to learn that during these two months they'd been mad with worry and had searched for me everywhere.) I walked up through the forest to the highway. At the gas station I approached a car, said that I was a student who needed to get to Ankara, and they agreed to give me a ride. A pilot named Koparal was driving, and his mother was sitting in the backseat.

I called a friend in Ankara, and we agreed to meet outside a movie theater. There I noticed my uncle in the crowd. I realized my friend had turned me in, and I started to run. My uncle chased me and caught me.

We went home. My parents and my three siblings were seated at the table. They were about to begin eating. My father glanced at me out of the corner of his eye, then turned to my mother and said, "Şükriye, could you please put out another plate?" I can't describe how ashamed I felt throughout that meal; I wanted to sink through the floor. My younger siblings gave me strange glances and looked me up and down, but they didn't have the courage to say anything. Not a word was uttered during the meal, and my family punished me with silence. Later everything returned to normal. For a time I did nothing but study; I was able to take makeup tests and to graduate. Eskihisar and Hannibal became memories of childish adventure. But the sea and Hemingway continued to have an important place in my life. This book is the result of that passion—I wrote it out of respect for Papa. Because without knowing it, he changed the life of a boy in Ankara who loved to read books.

The Fisherman and His Son

The sea was sleeping, motionless, but soon it would be woken by a slight breeze. The breeze that began before daybreak eased the pain in the fisherman's legs, which had been aching for hours from the damp night air. It was time to get up; the dark blue of the sea was taking on a strange whiteness. The sky was different every day; you looked and it was purple, then it was pink, then milk white, then it would turn a host of colors that would glisten as they were reflected on the mirror surface of the sea.

The fisherman hadn't missed the waking of the sea in thirty years. He got up every day before sunrise, drank a small glass of olive oil, then set out for the fishing harbor. He'd learned about drinking olive oil on an empty stomach from the healthy elders of the village who'd lived past a hundred. The elders who pressed the olives from the centuries-old trees whose trunks were as gnarled as their own bodies.

When he reached the harbor it was already light, but the dirt road was deserted. No one went out as early as he did. This suited the fisherman, who didn't talk much and preferred solitude. He was a tall, thin man. His sunken cheeks, grayish hazel eyes, and tousled, sandy hair gave his face a handsomeness that no one noticed, envied, or thought about. He had the body of a man who worked for a living; he didn't look at all like the city dwellers, whose bodies grow round from inactivity and overeating. He had an air that would seem wild to them, a bit too masculine, indeed even tough. These people had so many things swirling through their minds, their intuition was overdeveloped and they struggled constantly to understand their anxieties. They would have trouble living in a village like this. Life was hard here, it was difficult, you couldn't stay on your feet without struggling to the point of exhaustion. Men, women, and even children had to adopt an attitude of resignation.

Mustafa never asked anything of anyone. And he would get angry at those who asked for bait, hooks, and lines when they went out fishing. If I can do my job well, he thought, so can everyone else. When Captain Tahsin, the master he'd worked with as a child, went into decline and retired, he'd made a down payment on his beautiful old motorboat, and he'd worked hard to make his payments. It bore the traces of thirty years of work: worn-out oars with blackened handles, the tiller and gunwales scored by fishing lines, and a hatch cover that rattled wildly when the motor was running. Traces of his master's hands and his own hands. His tanned and leathery hands looked like two powerful sea creatures that were independent of him.

As he did every morning, he untied the boat, jumped in, and said *In the name of God* aloud. The motor that had served him well over the years started at once; it never gave him any trouble. As always, the sound of the motor ringing out across the bay invigorated him. The sea was calm, and the boat glided out of the harbor. Of course it was always like that at this hour, but soon there would be slight turbulence; as the sun rose the sea would grow irritable and waves would begin to form. In the afternoon it would swell with the harsh wind like a jealous lover.

He turned on the little radio he always kept in the boat, and a poignant Aegean folk song began to play: *The masts of the ships are tall / The "efe's" heart is stout.* The music from the radio, Aegean folk songs, mournful

3

tunes, and lively dances, kept him company until he finished work and returned to the village. To his surprise, his father's favorite song came on. *You never became a bride and I never became a groom / That's why I always stare off into the distance.*

His father had been a poor fisherman who was consumed by the sea. In those days there were no tourists yet, and fish was both plentiful and cheap, but the fish they caught didn't provide enough for them to live on. Fish was dirt cheap. Fish was more expensive now—squid, octopus, mussels, and shrimp sold for high prices, but the sea provided less than it used to. Their trawl lines brought in less than they once did. Large, sonar-equipped ships from far away, from other seas, scraped the bottom of the sea. Expensive restaurants had opened along the shore, and they competed for the freshest fish. The people who caught the fish would never step foot in those places. The prices were just too high. People from Istanbul came and spent in a single evening what the villagers earned in a month, that's what they said. There were also those who said *they spend that much for a drink in a luxury hotel.* In any event, the villagers couldn't even contemplate eating fish in a restaurant. It seemed like a strange idea. The restaurants were good customers, but the fishermen still barely got by.

Mustafa always remembered his father's hands. Huge, shapeless, hard, ludicrous, almost inhuman. Touching his hand was like touching a tree. Now his hands had become like his father's. His late father had been a hard man, a chain smoker, and lung cancer brought him an early death. He'd sold his old boat to pay off his debts.

The sound of the motor reached the sleeping houses on the bay, then spread toward the far shore. For three days a storm had whipped up the sea. It had battered the shore, but now it was tranquil. There was no trace of it, except for the flotsam that swirled lazily along the shore. The sea would slowly sweep it all away. But this flotsam was only of concern to the tourists; the fishermen wouldn't swim unless they had to.

The years had made him part of the sea, as if he were seaweed, a fish, a rock, sand, or pebbles. He breathed in unison with the sea: if the sea was rough he was rough, if it was still he was still, if it was tranquil he was tranquil. He was generally a quiet man; he didn't talk unless he needed to. He always had a cigarette behind his ear as he repaired his nets, washed his boat, or stared into the depths. He didn't go to the coffeehouse like the other fishermen, he wouldn't play cards, and in the evening he wouldn't drink anywhere except home. The old fishermen who'd known him since childhood said he'd always been a calm man, that when his seven-year-old son Deniz drowned he'd retreated further into himself. He'd gone out to sea with his son one day, and after he returned without him he was a broken man. He no longer even spoke to his wife, who sobbed and beat her chest all day.

One night he turned and said to his wife, "Deniz was taken by the sea, perhaps he knows something." Did she blame him? Did she ever wonder why he hadn't saved her son? She never said anything about this to him. It was as if even the young woman's color changed after losing her son. Her face, her expression, the light in her green eyes, everything about her had faded. When she wasn't crying she looked like a flower that hadn't been watered. Her head was bowed, and she looked as if she'd fall apart if you touched her. For a long time after this terrible loss, they didn't even look at each other. There was no longer even the slightest expression of emotion. They no longer reminded each other about what had to be done or thought about, they blamed each other for even existing, and they only spoke about the most essential aspects of daily life. The house became a minefield, and even the smallest mistake inevitably led to an explosion. If it went any further, there would be no return.

The boy's body was never found. The idea of not thinking about that stormy day, of forgetting, seemed like betrayal to him. Every night when he lay his head on his pillow he relived even the most painful details. He kept scratching at the scab and reopening the wound. It seemed shameful to continue to live after his son had died. His regret was as fresh as it had been on the first day. If he didn't know that it was the greatest sin, he would have drowned himself in those wild waters.

Again and again he remembered waking early that morning with his son, who was so fond of the sea. The delight in the seven-year-old's eyes as the boat moved out to sea, watching him lean over the side and trail his tiny fingers in the water, the way he shouted "Father, look, look," how the boy looked up in gratitude when he told him to be careful, then dark clouds covering the sky, that cool wind, the storm that blew up on the open sea, the boat being tossed about like a walnut shell, then capsizing when a wave struck from the side, clinging to the overturned boat, looking around for his son but not being able to see him, diving again and again into the raging sea. He looked for him for hours in that stormy sea, checking the nets in the water in case he'd been caught in them, beseeching God for help all the while. Afterward he searched for days in the hope of at least finding the body, but he found not even a trace. He searched every patch of seaweed, every rock, every trench, every mysterious cave; he saw every kind of fish and octopus, sea creatures great and small; he swam with them but he couldn't find his son.

Since then no one had heard him speak of what had happened. He'd always been a taciturn man, but it seemed as if he felt that any word he uttered would be disrespectful to his son, and he retreated into himself. He was like a tortoise. He didn't even speak to his wife; after eating in silence he would go to bed early. What they did some nights couldn't be called "making love." Their young bodies sought what they needed in the same manner they ate dinner in silence. In the morning, he would get up and go to his boat while his wife was still sleeping. His friends liked him; they were accustomed to his disposition. They said cigarettes were his closest friend, then knocked on wood and prayed to be spared the pain of losing a child themselves.

Seamen believe in luck, because they never know what the vast sea has in store for them, what blessings or disasters await them. They know that water, wind, clouds, lightning, and waves are powerful, and that people are helpless; they have more respect for nature than city dwellers do. And when they think about the sea, they don't think only of the surface, as city dwellers do, but of the exciting and distinctive world beneath, full of both bounty and danger. Even the simplest, barely literate fisherman with no knowledge of mythology has a sense of the nature of Poseidon. At times the vast sea grows mad with anger and becomes an unstoppable force as it attacks with its trident, and sometimes it becomes a compliant lover and strokes your face with sweet breezes, apologizing for its vengeful days. It is the source of both bounty and calamity. The blue that everyone sees is the skin of this gigantic body, and the movement that begins with the wind is the sea's awakening.

Mustafa knew the sea well because he'd been a diver in his youth. He knew the seaweeds that danced so slowly to their own rhythm, and those strange creatures that only existed underwater. Once he hadn't had the heart to spear two groupers he'd found in the hollow of a rock, and on every dive after that they seemed to greet him. They had never fled from him, perhaps because they'd become accustomed to him.

Mustafa had decided that the larger of the groupers was named Osman. As a young man playing cards with his friends in the coffeehouse, he'd made everyone laugh when he said one of them was named Osman, but he didn't know the other's name. Later, he didn't understand why everyone had laughed. No one realized that this quiet fisherman wasn't joking. He would never harm a protected species. He was being completely serious. Cats and dogs had names, so why shouldn't fish? After losing his son he stopped diving and going to the coffeehouse. He didn't know what became of Osman and the other grouper.

The sea was a workplace, it was life, it was a lover, it was cruel, calm, lovable, angry. Sometimes the sea caused him pain, and sometimes it was generous. The sea didn't surrender herself to everyone who cast a line or spread a net. Of course you had to know every species' season, habitat, migration routes; the right hook to use; the right bait; the right way to catch it. Sometimes an inexperienced fisherman might have beginner's luck and land a red gurnard, but this happened only rarely.

Sometimes tourists wanted to experience the excitement of fishing, and they paid well. It was clear from the start that they were less interested in fishing than in excitement. They didn't have to fish for a living. Most of them were decent people, but some of them talked too much and irritated the fishermen with meaningless questions. As if they could learn a lifetime of experience in a single trip. When a fish bit they got excited and jumped to their feet, and the boat rocked wildly. Mustafa would move them from place to place. He never brought them to his own rocks, to his own secret fishing spots. He left things completely to chance.

Recently there had been a lot of fish near the fish farms that were ruining the bay. They were either fish that had escaped the nets or larger fish that were attracted by the feed. Sometimes as they were looking for feed they got caught in the nets and ended up being eaten themselves. Mustafa felt sorry for these fish. If he saw them in time and circumstances permitted, he would dive and free them. Especially if it was a dolphin. Mustafa loved dolphins like brothers. He thought they understood he was a friend. Sometimes, when he was bringing tourists around, the dolphins would swim close to the boat, jumping and frolicking, and everyone would admire them. Then the tourists would give bigger tips, especially if they were able to get a photograph.

One day a curious tourist showed him a book and asked him if he'd read it. He laughed bitterly. "When do I have time for books, I barely make ends meet," he said, looking at the book as if it were a strange object. But the tourist insisted.

"This book is about a fisherman like you. It's a novel by an American writer. Are there swordfish around here, do you fish for them?"

"Of course," said Mustafa, "I fish for whatever there is, whatever God ordains."

"Look," said the tourist, "the fisherman in the novel isn't young like you, he's an old man. One day he catches a huge swordfish with a lure, and he starts trying to pull it into his boat. You see, the fish is so big he has to struggle for days and nights—the old man's hands are covered in blisters and wounds. He's hungry, but he keeps going. Finally the fish gets tired, and he kills it with a spear. The fish is too big to get into the boat, so he ties it to the side with a rope. Then he heads back, but what do you think happens on the way?"

Irritably, Mustafa said, "The man wasn't a good fisherman. I don't like him."

The tourist was surprised, but he continued. "Listen, we're just getting to the exciting part, on the way back, sharks begin eating that huge fish..."

Mustafa interrupted him. "Forget it, sir, forget it. I don't like the man, this story isn't for me, he wasn't a good fisherman."

The tourist realized he wasn't going to get through to Mustafa, but it did occur to him to ask why he didn't like the old fisherman. "If that fish was so wonderful, if it struggled for its life for days, he should have cut the line and said, *Go, my lion, you deserve to live, may the sea bless you.* Sometimes you catch a huge fish, sir, you come eye to eye with it as you pull it into the boat, and it looks at you so pitifully you can't bear to kill it, so you throw it back into the sea."

Most fishermen don't bother to retrieve lost nets, they just buy new ones, but these plastic nets get tangled in the rocks on the sea floor, and they harm the sea and the fish. This was why Mustafa would dive to retrieve them. He even retrieved the nets other fishermen had left behind—he looked at these fishermen with rebuke. Mustafa remembered the time before plastic nets; he liked that better. Everyone pulled up their rope nets carefully, then brought them ashore, stuck a thumb in a hole, and stretched them in order to repair them. The nets would smell deeply of the sea.

Depending on the season, there would be sea bass; perch; *lampuki*, whose strung bodies strained fishing rods; glistening seabream; red mullet, queen of the fishes, whose wet scales, glistening with pink, always amazed the fisherman. *Excuse me, brother,* he would say, *these are the rules of nature, I hunt you, but you hunt other fish, this is how the world works.* Mustafa had often seen big fish open their mouths monstrously wide and suck up hundreds of small fish. The tiny fish tried to swarm together to escape, but they never succeeded.

As the other fishermen returned to the shore, they thought Mustafa was talking to himself in his boat. In fact. he was talking to the fish. He had observed the sea for so long that it was as if he had become one with it.

Recently Mustafa had noticed that the sea had changed. They no longer heard the names of fish they'd known in their grandparents' time; they'd begun seeing strangely shaped fish. One of them was called the "puffer fish," and all the fishermen had learned that it can be fatal to eat. But they liked the lionfish, which they'd never encountered before: it was delicious. The spines were poisonous, so you had to be careful when handling it and cleaning it. Neither their parents nor their grandparents knew where these fish had come from, but curious fishermen had heard various explanations. Some said these strange fish were appearing because the seas were getting warmer; some said they'd come in the bilges of foreign ships, or else their eggs had.

*T*hen a professor from the fisheries department of an urban university came and gathered them all together. "Gentlemen," he said, "these are invasive species of fish, and if we don't do something they'll wipe out all the local fish. They came to the Mediterranean from the Indian Ocean through the Suez Canal. Then they multiply here. When large freighters return from the Red Sea, they take on water for ballast, and then they let the water out when they arrive here. This is how their eggs spread through our waters."

The bespectacled, goateed professor came every month to teach the fishermen. He'd been appointed by the fisheries department. He was a scholar. He told them the real names of all the fish they knew. These names were in a foreign language; there was no way they could remember them.

They were distressed by what the professor told them. They looked at each other and mumbled about how bad things were. They thought that the people who had cut down the forest to build ugly housing developments, who built hotels on landfill, who gouged the mountains for metals, were going to take the sea away from them as well. They'd never had to think about protecting the village of their parents and grandparents. Because in the old days, no one ever harmed the trees, the air, or the sea. It would never even have occurred to them. They watched in anger as people from elsewhere aggressively seized nature. They talked about this in the coffeehouse every day. Some said:

"The company that cut down the forest on the mountain is going to mine for gold, and they're going to do it with a poison called cyanide. It will seep into the groundwater and give us all cancer."

Then they all began talking at once:

"But this place is already gold, the water and the air are gold."

"What need is there to dig holes in the mountains?"

"The flooding in the mountains last winter, we'd never seen anything like that."

"No, we never had floods like that before."

"Those bastards cut down the trees, and the water just rushed down."

Yes, but wasn't this their own property, hadn't the village been handed down to them by their ancestors? What business did these people have here? A fisherman who'd flown to Istanbul when a relative was ill said, "If you saw our coast from the air it would make you cry. Bays full of fish farms; there's green sludge everywhere; it's because of all the chemicals and the artificial feed."

"Weren't these farms supposed to be in the open sea? That's what they told us."

"The mining companies lied to us too."

"We're dying, and there's no one left to mourn us. Who's going to listen to some poor villagers?"

Mustafa saw the ever-growing fish farms as fish prisons. He felt sorry for the fish prisoners. The fish they caught had at least enjoyed the freedom of the sea, had fulfilled their destinies, but these fish went straight from captivity to the frying pan. Then these puffer fish appeared. This was the most immediate threat. This monstrous fish was threatening their livelihoods.

Sari Yusuf, with whom Mustafa and Mesude had been friends since childhood, used to say:

"This puffer fish is a very strange creature. It can chew a can—I've seen it with my own eyes. It can tear apart a cola can."

The other fishermen all said that puffer fish had cut their nets, that they weren't leaving any other fish in the sea. They complained that their nets were all coming up full of these poisonous fish. One of them said, "With God as my witness, the other day I pulled up four hundred of them. I didn't know what to do. Should I burn them or bury them?"

The expert professor said, "Never do anything like that, in fact it's against the law to bring those fish ashore. After they're dead, cut off their tails and throw them back into the sea. If you bury them, animals might try to dig them up and eat them."

Then the fishermen wondered about the creatures in the sea—what would happen when they ate these fish? And they didn't understand the part about the tails. Why should they cut off the tails? The professor said, "The government will announce a decision very soon. They're going to pay fishermen five lira for each tail."

Again the fishermen looked at each other. They began calculating how much they would get for four hundred fish tails. Of course the puffer fish were harmful to them and their equipment, but the money wasn't bad. The fishermen would sell the larger, more expensive fish to the restaurants they had agreements with. They sold the small fish from the red counters by the shore to the locals to buy cheaply. This was what they themselves ate. The others were for wealthy people.

When Mustafa returned from the sea and tied up his boat, he saw Ömer, the only person in the village whom everyone liked.

"Why do you set out so early every day?" Ömer asked the fisherman.

"That's what I always do," said Mustafa, "I always set out early."

"Don't go out so early; if you do I'll get angry," said Ömer in a stern tone. He frowned.

"Why shouldn't I go out, Ömer, what harm will it do you?"

"Then I can't give you the pearls. My mother doesn't want me to go out that early. And I have to milk the goats at that hour."

"What pearls?" asked Mustafa.

T he mere sight of Ömer put a smile on everyone's face. His head was huge, his arms were short, and his hands were tiny. He looked at people as if he lived his life underwater, with those beautiful but expressionless eyes. It was the result of inbreeding; he was a very likable boy. He was about sixteen or seventeen years old.

His swollen eyelids gave him a strange expression. "That's very rude, very rude," he lisped, and shook his head.

Mustafa was in a bad mood, but it always did him good to talk to Ömer. It cheered him up a little.

"What are you thinking?" shouted Ömer. "How many times have I told you?"

"What did you tell me, Ömer?"

"When you went out fishing I was going to give you little pearls, and you were going to throw them into the sea. The fish would swallow them, and they would grow in their stomachs."

"Ahhh, sorry, Ömer, I completely forgot," said Mustafa. But Ömer had never said anything like that to him. So Ömer had a new fixation. He would get strange ideas from time to time. Before the pearls, he'd thought it was essential to go to the mayor every morning to get his forehead stamped. Suddenly he would become a government official. He would show people his forehead and admonish them to behave. He would make a sound as if he were blowing a whistle and say, "Behave yourself or you'll go straight to jail."

"Have you told your friends?"

"Yes, every morning I give them a handful of pearls. They take them. You're the only person who isn't helping."

"I swear I forgot, I'm sorry, Ömer."

"It's your fault we're not rich," shouted the boy.

"I'll tell you what we can do. Since I go out early you might not see me. Give me those pearls now, and I'll throw them in the sea tomorrow."

Ömer looked at him with a strange smile. Then he said, "Fine, I'll go get them." Then he gave him a long look. "Don't go anywhere," he said.

"Don't worry," said Mustafa, "I'll be right here."

Ömer ran off. He came back with his hands in the pocket of the jacket he wore winter and summer.

"Here," he said.

He took a handful of small, white pebbles out of his pocket.

"Take these."

"Thanks, Ömer."

"Throw them in the sea tomorrow morning."

"I will."

"But don't forget ..."

"I won't forget."

"Throw them at the big fish."

"I will, Ömer, don't worry." He could see that the boy was pleased.

Sometimes no one has any childish imagination, he thought. Once he'd seen him buy salt from the grocery store and dump it into the sea. When they asked him why, he said, *There wasn't enough salt in the sea so I added some*, then, *If it weren't for me no one would take care of anything around here.* He was a wonderful boy. Sometimes Seyit Efendi, who raised animals in his garden and decorated them with gongs and bells and brightly colored cloth so the tourists could ride them, would put Ömer on his beautiful camel's back. The boy would giggle in delight.

reen seaweed, white clouds, white gulls, wet, purplish rocks, purple mountains in the distance, barren islands...As he glided toward the secret rock that he regarded as his own property, and that the other fisherman silently accepted as such, one hand on the tiller, drawing deeply from the cigarette in his other hand, he saw something in the distance. It looked like a person swimming, but it couldn't be, because it was too far out; no one would swim this far from the shore. He steered the boat toward the object and increased his speed. Sometimes logs fell off freighters. Sometimes when yacht captains on autopilot weren't careful, especially in the dark, they could run into them and, God forbid, even sink. If this object was a log, it could pose a danger to other boats.

As he sped toward the object, he realized it wasn't a log. It looked like a person, face in the water, moving with the sea. As he drew a bit closer, he no longer had any doubt. Yes, it was a woman. She was wearing a black dress, her long, black hair was spread out around her head, her arms were open, her face was in the water, it was clear she had drowned. Mustafa approached carefully, took her by the shoulder, and turned her over. He'd been right, the dark-skinned young woman's face was slightly swollen and beginning to go purple; she'd drowned. Mustafa was perplexed. Who was this woman, why was she so far out to sea, had she fallen off a ship? Then he remembered the fierce storm that had broken out during the night. She must have been one of the migrants who frequently tried to reach the Greek islands in inflatable boats. Wherever the boat sank, the storm must have carried her there. The islands of Kos, Kalimnos, and Leros were quite close.

He thought about what to do with the woman. He couldn't just leave her there, with no grave. People should be buried when they die, everyone had that right, but in recent times thousands of refugees had been left to disappear in the sea. He couldn't bring himself to leave this woman without a grave. He took out the old cell phone he seldom used and carried only in case of emergency, but he saw that there was no signal. It would be difficult to get the woman into the boat, but she was small, so he decided to try. There were no rocks or islands nearby where he could leave her while he went to inform the coast guard.

He leaned down, held the woman under her arms, and started to pull. She was small, but the water had made her heavier, and it was difficult. After considerable struggle he managed to get her halfway into the boat; her long, wet hair was plastered across her face. Once her upper body was in the boat it was easier to pull the rest of her in. Her head was slumped next to the hold, and her thin body was curled up in the hull. She looked younger lying there in the boat; she must have been in her early twenties. Even her thin fingers had turned purple. Mustafa hoped that a cigarette would ease his aching heart. He dried his hands, lit a cigarette, and inhaled dolefully as he turned the boat toward the bay. In any event, he was in no state to catch fish that day.

On the way back he looked at the woman's face and tried to guess where she was from. He guessed that she was from someplace like Syria, Pakistan, or Afghanistan. Then, thinking that it was sinful to look at her like that even though she was dead, he covered her with a tarpaulin. He let go of the tiller while he was doing this, but as soon as he raised his head he saw that he was about to hit another dead body, so he turned the rudder hard to the right. Then he turned and approached slowly. There was another person in the sea. It was a man, bobbing in the boat's wake, his face in the water, his arms open. He was wearing a blue jacket and he had dark hair. Mustafa turned him over, and when he saw the man, dark-skinned, with dark, curly hair, already turning purple, he guessed that like the woman he was in his early twenties. Perhaps he was the woman's husband, or brother, or other relative. Or perhaps a fellow citizen who had shared her fate. *I'll have to bring him into the boat too*, he thought, *there's no room, and even if they're dead it's shameful, sinful, to put them on top of each other. If the man isn't the woman's husband.* Then he thought of something. He tied a rope under the man's arms and got underway. The rope tensed, and the dead man was pulled along behind the boat.

It was clear that another refugee boat had capsized nearby. If that was the case, there should be more bodies. He thought about what he would do if he found a few more. He couldn't figure out what he would do. He only had one more rope, and of course the fishing lines. With these he could perhaps bring one or two more victims to shore. For a moment he thought about whether the fishing lines would be strong enough. Then he decided that they would be. There wouldn't be a strong fish struggling to free itself on the other end. Bodies being towed slowly wouldn't present a problem.

As the boat moved slowly and respectfully, like a hearse, he saw dolphins and grew anxious. He worried that if these playful friends got up to their usual games, swimming under the boat and emerging on the other side, leaping out next to the boat and spraying it with water, it would disturb the dead. But amazingly the dolphins were calm that day, as if they understood the situation. They swam calmly around the boat and the body being towed behind it. Their dark-blue bodies glowed in the clear water.

Then Mustafa saw the large dolphin he considered his true friend, the one he called Father, approaching in all his magnificence. Father approached slowly, pushing something brightly colored with his nose. The dolphin pushed this object, which looked like a plastic life preserver, as far as the boat, and then Mustafa was amazed. There was a baby in a small inflatable boat. The baby was motionless, its eyes were closed, and its face was purple. It had been tied to the boat. Mustafa's heart began beating faster, and his breathing quickened. He thought God must be testing him. Before he had time to grasp or even think about what was happening, he sensed that this was a miracle that was going to change his life forever. He leaned down, untied the baby, and took its tiny body in his arms. Then all the dolphins, including Father, moved off with leaps and bounds as if they were celebrating a victory. Mustafa wanted to put the baby down in the boat but he couldn't. He brought the purple face close to him, as if he wanted to warm it. It must have been in the sun too long, because its face was burning. The baby was also dark-skinned. It couldn't have been more than two months old. Perhaps this was the dead woman's child, perhaps he was carrying a family. Without putting the baby down, he sped toward the shore.

Then, as if by a miracle, the baby let out a faint moan. Its lips seemed to quiver. With difficulty, he managed to bring fresh water to the baby's lips with a ladle. Then he took out a clean handkerchief, wet it, and got the baby to suck water. The baby's eyes were closed, it was feeble and exhausted, but it began sucking water from the cloth. It sucked so slowly that you wouldn't have noticed it unless you watched carefully. Mustafa cleaned the baby's face, washed off the salt water. Without letting go of the baby, he raced the boat as fast as it could go. As the boat sped through the calm water, Mustafa looked back. The dead body was moving like a water-skier, there was no problem. Even if there had been a problem, it was more important to save the baby.

Unfortunately there was nothing in the boat to feed the baby. As he looked around in desperation, he found some milk chocolate that one of the tourists had left behind. *Will the baby be able to swallow this*, he wondered, *perhaps it's better to let it melt in the sun.* He grabbed a small pan that was hot from sitting in the sun. When he was at sea for a long time, he would use the pan to cook fish over a propane stove. He couldn't take the stove out and light it now. The chocolate began to melt as soon as he put it in the pan. He was pleased. He dipped his forefinger into the melted chocolate and brought it to the baby's lips. After he did this several times, the baby began to move slightly. Its lips moved as if it wanted to suck the chocolate-covered finger. This was enough to make the fisherman's heart swell and his eyes fill with tears. He muttered a prayer.

Meanwhile the village had come into view. He'd be there in four or five minutes. He took out his phone; he had a signal now. He called the coast guard. He explained the situation to Petty Officer Talat. *I'm bringing the bodies of two refugees*, he said, *they drowned, poor things.* He hadn't found it necessary to mention the baby. In any event, he was going to hand him over in a few minutes. The fisherman became pensive. Was he really going to hand the baby over? Should he? By law of course he had to, but then he looked at the little baby, at the tiny lips trying to suck his finger. He saw that the coast guard was waiting for him on the shore. He would be entering the harbor soon. Suddenly, without being fully aware of what he was doing, he placed the baby under the deckhead and covered it with a tarpaulin. He slowed down and entered the harbor. Curious onlookers had gathered on the shore. As he was mooring, Petty Officer Talat asked him impatiently what had happened. Mustafa told him. "One body is here and the other is at the end of that rope." The men had already seen the situation and were wading into the water to retrieve the man's body. The petty officer asked him if there was anyone else, and he said no, he hadn't seen anyone else. "There have to be more of them," said the petty officer as he ordered his men to begin a search. "How many does this make? The sea is full of death around here, all we do these days is pull bodies out of the sea and chase the smugglers." Then, turning to Mustafa, he said, "After you make your report, go to the prosecutor and give him your statement." Mustafa nodded. When the commander boarded the coast guard boat the ropes were untied, the powerful motor started, and the boat moved off with a roar. The crowd began to disperse slowly. Some were watching the powerful boat, some were watching the ambulance that was taking away the bodies. These were people Mustafa only knew by sight—his fisher-men friends were all out at sea.

Mustafa waited until people lost interest in him. It was difficult not to check on the baby, but he had to be patient. He told the police what had happened; then they filed a report and left. When Mustafa saw that there was no one near the boat, he carefully placed the baby in a wicker basket. He covered the baby with his undershirt and set off for home. When he passed the policemen he said, "I'm just going to go home and clean up a little, then I'll go see the prosecutor." "Fine," said the policeman. "The prosecutor is about to go on his lunch break, and you can make your statement when he comes back." He nodded at the people who wanted to talk to him and rushed toward his two-room house near the top of the hill, overlooking the sea.

The house had been left to him by his father. When his father had died an early death, his mother moved in with her daughter, who had married a bank clerk in Nazilli. Thankfully they were doing well. They'd had word Filiz was pregnant, and they were counting the days. His older brother Salim had never taken to fish-ing and was running a teahouse in Aydın.

Mustafa wanted to run home, but he forced him-self to slow down so as not to attract attention. He fi-nally reached the whitewashed house that stood apart from the other houses. Mesude was shelling beans on a bench in the garden.

"What happened," she asked, "I hope there's nothing wrong."

"No, no," said Mustafa, "come inside."

When they entered the living room Mustafa took the baby out of the basket.

"Who's this baby?" asked Mesude.

"Deniz," said Mustafa.

"What do you mean? His name is Deniz too?"

"I named him. I named him on the way here. The sea took our Deniz but later it gave us another Deniz. I'll tell you the story, but first we have to bring this baby back to life. There's milk in the house, isn't there?"

Of course there was; every two or three days Mesude bought a bucket of milk from their neighbor Seyit Efendi, who had cows, dogs, chickens, and a camel, and who talked to his animals all day.

"But how will we get him to drink it? The baby looks dead, are you sure it's alive?"

They didn't know what to do.

Mustafa said, "We need a baby bottle, but I can't go to the pharmacy to buy one because they'll get suspicious."

Mesude looked confused. She went into the kitchen. He heard her run the water, and then she came back with a baby bottle full of milk. "I couldn't bring myself to throw anything away," she said, looking straight ahead. "Oh," Mustafa said softly.

Mesude took the baby in her arms and tried to put the bottle in its mouth, but the baby's lips didn't move. "Oh no," said Mustafa, but Mesude told him not to worry, and the baby began to suck. Feebly, but with a will to hang on to life.

*I*n the afternoon Mustafa boarded the municipal bus that went to the town. It took half an hour. On one side there was a slope covered with pine trees; on the other side, at the foot of a cliff, the white-specked sea washed against the shore. It was as if the fierce storm of the previous night had never occurred. The sea was so calm.

One day, when Deniz was watching the surf roll onto the shore, he'd said, "Look, Father, the sea's hair has become curly." That day Mustafa had laughed at these words, but remembering them now made him feel bad. He was angry at the sea now. He continued to make his living from it, but he was nagged by questions about why it had taken his son from him, why it hadn't spared him.

The town was full of German and English tourists, as it was every summer. Their white arms turned as red as lobsters in the afternoon sun. Mustafa tried not to look at the tourist girls, because they went around half naked, but he couldn't help glancing from time to time.

It was unbearably hot in the courthouse. The officials were working in short-sleeved shirts, but there was an air conditioner in the prosecutor's office. Mustafa was uneasy when he stepped into the office; he thought the air-conditioning could make people sick. Of course it got hot in summer, but why make the room as cold as winter? These city dwellers were strange people. He himself never got sick, but there was a baby now, and he had to be more careful. He pictured the baby's face; he hadn't even seen his eyes yet.

The prosecutor was a young, slightly built man with wire-frame glasses. He looked like an irritable person. Behind his desk hung a red cloth that had been stretched and framed. A young woman sat at a computer in front of the desk. At first the prosecutor didn't look up from the papers he was reading. Then he looked up at Mustafa.

"Are you Mustafa Sılacı?" he asked. "According to the report, you found the bodies of two refugees."

"Yes, that's correct," said Mustafa.

"Why don't you tell me what happened."

Mustafa told him everything that had happened, except for the baby: time, location, all the details. The young woman wrote everything he said on the computer.

"You didn't see anyone else?"

"No, sir, I didn't see anyone else."

"Fine," said the prosecutor, "After you sign this statement you can go."

He didn't hesitate to sign the statement. He'd succeeded in convincing himself he hadn't seen anyone else. There definitely hadn't been anyone else.

When he got home it was like the old days. Mesude had laid the baby at her feet and was rocking it gently. The baby had been washed and powdered and partly swaddled and was sleeping peacefully, as if he hadn't faced death on the open sea. When Mesude asked him what he'd told the prosecutor, Mustafa said, "Nothing. I told him I'd found two people in the sea. I didn't mention the baby."

"Fine, but isn't this against the law? How can we not tell the authorities about the baby?"

Mustafa didn't say anything. His wife continued, "I understand you, Mustafa, don't think I don't.
I've warmed to the baby too. He's such a tiny thing,
smaller than the sea bass you catch. But he isn't ours,
and if the authorities find out we have him they'll
throw us in jail."

"We won't tell them, said Mustafa. "We won't tell
anyone."

"You want this baby so much you're not thinking
straight. How can you hide a baby? We might manage
for a few days, but then what? Isn't everyone going to
wonder where this baby came from?"

"But I've already given my statement. I said I didn't
see anyone else—I can't go back on that."

"We'll find a way out. You can say, I don't know,
you can say you found him later, or that you thought
he was dead."

"Let's think about it for a couple of days. Look,
who can we give the baby to when he's in this state,
he's half-dead, let's bring him back to life, then we'll
think things over. Meanwhile, try to not let on to the
neighbors. They won't hear anything. After all, he's
too weak to even cry."

Just then the baby sighed and they both forgot the
argument. They looked at the baby in silence.

That night Mustafa dreamt about the father dolphin. The dolphin had come up to his boat and was trying to tell him something, but Mustafa didn't understand.

"What are you saying? I don't understand."

When the baby opened his eyes for the first time, Mustafa and Mesude were beside themselves with delight, as if all of nature had flowered and the almond trees were covered in white blossoms. The new Deniz had black eyes, whereas their own Deniz had had hazel eyes, but they both had the same innocent gaze. Just like all babies.

Mesude alternated between delight and surprise. Just when she'd thought that after Deniz she would never take another child in her arms, here she was holding this beautiful baby. She couldn't get enough of his black eyes, of the sounds he made, of his smell, of the way he waved his hands in the air. She sang the lullabies she used to sing to their Deniz.

If it were up to Mustafa he would never have left the house, he would have watched the baby day and night, but he had to make a living and he didn't want the neighbors to get suspicious, so every morning at daybreak he got into his boat and went out to sea. On his first trip out after the incident, after dropping anchor and casting his nets, he rose to his feet, opened his arms to the sky, and said aloud, "Thanks, God. Thanks. Your ways are unfathomable. Thanks."

Mustafa had his own manner of praying. The *khojas* in the village had warned him several times that you don't say thanks to God, you say "Praise God" or "My gratitude is eternal." But Mustafa continued to speak to God in his own manner; he thought it was truer. When Deniz was taken from him he had resented God, he hadn't spoken to him in years, and he'd even stopped going to the holiday prayers he'd gone to since childhood. He used to complain to himself, "When there are so many wicked people in this world, why did He have to take my son?" but he never addressed God directly. When Mesude said, "Don't do this, Mustafa, don't anger God, you're committing a sin," he would tell her to be quiet. He said, "He took my innocent child," to which she would respond, "Repent, repent, forgive him, God, he's lost his mind, he doesn't know what he's saying."

When he returned exhausted one evening, the shore smelled of fried fish and anise. Sometimes his fishermen friends would gather on the beach to cook fish and drink rakı. Because they knew his disposition, it would never occur to them to invite him to join them. That's why they were astounded when he walked over to them, pulled up a stool, and sat down. Scorpion fish and picarel were sizzling in a pan over a propane stove. The cats of the village had gathered in a wider circle around them, waiting and tensed for the chance to dart in like an arrow to steal some fish. They'd become so good at this that before you knew what was going on, they darted in like lightning and grabbed a fish—you didn't even see it. There was one orange cat who had become almost demonically skilled at this. No one could stop him. Everyone just let him take what he wanted. In any event, the fishermen would always give the cats their share, then sip their rakı. The cats also knew that they would get the scraps.

They saw Ömer waddling toward them. The boy showed them his cheeks. This time he'd had both cheeks stamped. This meant he'd remembered he was a government official. Someone had given him a whistle too. He took it out and blew it.

"Behave yourselves," he said, "or I'll throw you in jail."

They answered in unison, "We'll behave, commander."

After giving them a stern warning, he wandered off, blowing his whistle as he went.

*Ç*iroz filled a small glass halfway with rakı, added water, and handed it to Mustafa. As he took his first sip, he said, "Sorry you had to go through that, it could have happened to any of us. The coast guard pulls hundreds of corpses out of the sea, but they don't find them all. Yesterday I was passing Kos, you know that park next to the marina, there were hundreds of them gathered there. Those are the ones who made it without drowning. They make them wait out in the open. They bring them to the camps. The situation there is really bad. God help them. Let's be thankful we're living here. Who knows what troubles they face that they're willing to risk their lives for. Imagine, some of them even get into those boats with babies."

Hüseyin the Stutterer was eager to chime in. "B-b-b-bab-baby Ay-Ay-Aylan..." (Presumably he was going to talk about Baby Aylan, who had broken everyone's heart when he washed up on the beach in Gümüşlük.) Aykut didn't have the patience to wait and said, "You know, the one whose body washed up on the shore." Hüseyin gave him a hurt look, then nodded and took a drink of rakı.

Mustafa had a look of happiness on his face that his friends hadn't seen for years. The man with no appetite was eating fish with pleasure, that taciturn man was drinking and chatting, that morose man was smiling. The fishermen glanced at one another as if to ask what had happened to him.

Where the sea was deep, it was a dark navy blue. Closer to the shore it became turquoise, then it turned a clear, bright blue, and then finally became foam. The sea was so enticing that evening. The sun was setting rapidly behind Kalymnos. After the fish had been fried, the scent of jasmine, geranium. and laurel wafted to them from nearby gardens. But then something happened that spoiled Mustafa's mood. The conversation once again turned to the refugees. Later he didn't remember who started this, but it came up that the coast guard had found more bodies. He'd already heard this, so he didn't listen with much interest. Then the Stutterer struggled to get out the news that three people had been found alive. The others rushed to provide the details. Two men and a woman. One man had been found on the point of death on some rocks, the other man and a woman had washed up on a tiny island. They'd been brought to the public hospital, where they were still in critical condition.

Mustafa stood abruptly and told his friends that he had to get going.

They watched him walk off with a bag of fish swinging in his hand, then began talking about him behind his back. Çiroz had been telling the others for a long time that Mustafa wasn't deliberately being aloof, that he just wanted to be alone with his troubles. Now they were more prepared to believe this, and felt less resentful toward Mustafa.

As Mustafa picked up the baby and rocked it in his arms, he told his wife about what he'd heard. For her part, she was pleased to see him coming home a little late and in good cheer; she was thankful that this grim man seemed to be returning to normal. Everyone else's husband hung out and drank with their friends, but hers was the only one who sat at home in silence, like a barn owl. She listened to her husband but didn't share his worries.

"If they were rescued, that's good. What are they going to say, even if someone asks and they say there was a baby? How could a baby survive when so many people drowned, they would just add him to the list of the missing, don't get yourself worked up about it." Mesude wasn't concerned about this news, but she continued to have the worry she'd had from the beginning. "What you need to think about is what we're going to do with the baby. We should give him to the authorities. How are we going to raise a baby in this tiny place, how are we going to hide him, sooner or later everyone is going to find out."

Mustafa had always considered his wife to be a sensible person, and he valued her opinion. "You're right," he said, "we can't raise a child in secret. I'll think about it and come up with a solution."

That night Mustafa lay down next to his wife with a feeling he hadn't experienced in years. He made love to her in a way he hadn't for so long, in a way he'd almost forgotten. Her skin became an intoxicating elixir for him. Somewhat surprised, and with the unabated female passion of her thirty-year-old body, she breathed in the smell of male yearning. For the first time in years she moved without feeling guilt, and she responded naturally to her husband's caresses.

Later they lay next to each other without speaking. There was nothing to talk about. The baby Deniz was asleep in the cradle, and they lay silent and awake, their naked bodies touching. Then the baby made a faint sound, something between sighing and crying. Mesude got up, took the baby in her arms, and went into the kitchen. When she returned, Mustafa asked for the baby, took him in his arms, fed him from the baby bottle, and watched him greedily suck the milk. He lifted the baby and smelled his neck.

Mesude said, "Don't get too attached, Mustafa. It will be harder for you if they take him away from us." Then she said she was having two friends over for tea the following day. She didn't know what to do, she couldn't tell them not to come, but if they came they'd see the baby. She could hide him in the bedroom, but what would she say if he started crying? Finally she said, "Mustafa, this isn't going to work. I know it will be painful for you, but tomorrow you have to give the baby to the police. Go out to sea first, then come back and say you found the baby. Otherwise we'll still lose the baby, but we'll be in a lot of trouble."

Mustafa didn't say anything, but he knew he couldn't do this. "I'll find a way, I have to find a way."

The following day he returned early from fishing. He sat with the baby, lay down next to him, fed him with the bottle, changed his diaper. The friends who came for tea in the evening didn't see him. Only once did he make a slight sound. Mustafa immediately put the bottle in his mouth. The guests in the sitting room heard the sound. Mesude laughed and said,

"The cat, its leg was injured so I bandaged it, it's resting inside." Her friend was surprised: "What kind of cat is that, it sounded just like a baby." Then they all decided that yes, cats can sound just like babies.

They got through that situation. But the following day, when Mustafa was out fishing, there was a banging on the door, Mesude hid the baby in the bedroom, then almost fainted when she saw it was the police at the door. They asked if Mustafa was home, and she said no, he was out fishing. The police had known he probably wouldn't be home; they said he should come in as soon as possible—his statement was incomplete.

*L*ike many families in the village, Mustafa and Mesude's families had been forced to migrate from Crete. The Cretans knew the flora and fauna of the mountains. They collected the herbs and mushrooms that were in season; they cooked with ingredients no one else had ever heard of, like milk thistle, leaf mustard, nettles, morel, shepherd's purse, and yarrow; they seasoned their food with wild thyme, soapwort, sage, and mint. Their gardens produced lemons, tangerines, and olive oil.

In the days before the tourists started coming, when the rugged countryside could only be traversed by mule, and olive oil, sponges, and wine were transported by ship, the elders would tell stories and tales by the stove on cool evenings during the mild winter. How the cattle used to race down the slope to drink water at İncilipinar, how Murat shot his brother-in-law at a wedding in Karaova, how when Stavros the Greek was sent to Greece during the population exchange, his cat cried in front of his empty house for months, how the church bell used to ring in windy weather, how bountiful the sea used to be, how many fish they used to catch by the little island, how the salt they placed on the rocks in the evening would be completely dry the following day, how a mine from the war got caught in someone's net, how the police came and destroyed the German mine, and had the moaning heard in the unbelievers' cemetery been from a Greek soldier who'd been left behind there? Of course there were endless squabbles over inheritance. Whose property had been left to whom, how shares were divided, which nephew had ended up with which uncle's property, who ended up taking whom to court. This was what they talked about as they drank tea made from the sage they'd gathered in the mountains. Although they argued about whether some of their least-believable memories were actually true or not, they swore that the story of the warship was something they'd really witnessed.

One day the villagers woke to see a gigantic warship in their little bay; they later learned it was a destroyer and referred to it as a "dostuyer." This happened in Mustafa's grandfather's time, during World War II. Fortunately Turkey didn't take part in that war, but they were close enough to the Greek islands to witness the orange flashes as they were attacked by German planes and Italian warships. In that war the Germans and the Italians were on one side and the English and the Greeks were on the other. The villagers couldn't sleep at night because of the sounds of the bombardment. The sound of the dive-bombers was so loud they feared they might be bombed by mistake.

The "dostuyer" was huge, but there was something strange about it. Half of the ship was gone. The ship had been split in two, and only the stern remained. When they saw this half warship they expressed concern and began muttering prayers. Morning prayers weren't held that day, because the imam was down by the shore looking at this unbelievable half ship. Everyone kept wondering about the other half of the ship, and whether it had sunk.

The sailors and officers on the half ship were waving their arms and trying to say something. At times their voices could be heard on the shore. The older villagers who'd known Greek attempted to translate what they heard into Turkish. Hearing these words they hadn't used or heard since childhood awoke hazy memories of their Greek friends and neighbors, children they'd gone to school with, or played with in the streets and gone fishing with.

No one would have believed that one day the police would come and round up these neighbors, who were as much a part of the village as the sea, the earth, and the olive trees, these people who had never known any other home, and send them by ship to what was for them a foreign country. How they would be forced to leave the stone houses left to them by their ancestors, their furniture, their boats, nets, anchors, and grieving cats, never to see them again. Now, hearing these cries in Greek from the deck of the destroyer brought tears to their eyes. But perhaps this sadness wasn't on account of the friends who'd gone, it was realizing how far in the past their own childhoods were.

Years later, Mustafa asked the professor who came every month from the university to tell the fishermen whether this story was true. The professor said yes, it was true. In 1943, at the height of the war, an English-built destroyer of the Greek navy, the *Adrias*, hit a German mine. The ship split in two. The front half sank; nothing remained of it. Twenty-one Greek sailors who'd been in the engine room lost their lives, and all of those who survived were injured. Navigating by the stars, they guided the wreck through the night to reach this bay in Turkish territorial waters.

It's difficult to enter that bay, even in daylight with a normal boat. But miraculously the captain managed to bring the ship in. The leading citizens of the village boarded the ship. Most of them didn't know any Greek. They sent word to the city by telephone. First they carried the wounded ashore, then brought them to the camouflaged British hospital ship anchored in Bodrum. The hospital ship was concealed with tarpaulins so that German planes couldn't spot it.

Ali Çavuş's coffeehouse in the village became the headquarters and diplomatic center. The Turkish authorities and the British consuls used it as their base. The government in Ankara gave the ship twenty-four hours to leave Turkish territorial waters, but the ship was in no condition to leave: it was on the point of sinking. The British government asked for an extension, and the half ship remained in the bay for six months. They buried the dead in the cemetery outside the village that the villagers referred to as the unbelievers' cemetery. They held a ceremony and marked the graves with crosses. Captain Tumbas said that when the war was over, they would collect these remains and bury them in Greece.

Meanwhile, the villagers fed and looked after the survivors. The ship was safe, because they'd covered it. They worked at sealing off the hull with wood and tarred tarpaulins. One night at the beginning of January, the captain bade farewell to the villagers and set sail. To avoid being seen by German planes they sailed by night and hid in island bays by day. They had no anchor, so they had to moor themselves to the rocks. They finally managed to reach Alexandria, where they were greeted with great fanfare. Captain Tumbas was later given a medal and promoted to admiral.

The Stutterer, who loved to join conversations, managed to ask, "S-s-s-Wha-whaa-what hap-happened to the ce-cemetery?"

The goateed professor answered, "They did what they said they were going to do. When the war was over they held a ceremony and disinterred them, brought them to the ship, fired a salute, and then brought them to Greece."

The fishermen realized that the story was true, that their grandparents hadn't made it up. But they couldn't quite imagine a wrecked destroyer in their bay.

This also explained the legend of the soldier moaning in the cemetery every night. They must have accidentally left one poor soldier behind, and he wept every night because he'd been forsaken in this Muslim land. The poor man didn't even have anyone to pray for him. From then on, those with strong faith would pray for this soldier's soul when they heard the moaning from the cemetery on windy nights. After all, they were People of the Book as well, weren't they? Didn't Muslims go to the now-derelict Orthodox church to light candles to the Virgin Mary? If you passed the church at night, weren't there dozens of flames flickering in front of the icon? Hadn't it been the custom to ask Greek neighbors for the cakes they made on St. Basil's Day?

They learned a lot more from the professor than just about invasive fish species. Once they asked him about a man their elders had told them about, a man who was called "the Fisherman" even though he didn't have much to do with fishing. He'd been a professor as well. It seems he was the son of an important pasha in Istanbul. People said that he'd murdered his father, been thrown into prison, and then later sent into exile in Bodrum. He was a learned man, and a writer who was respected in foreign countries. Their grandparents had learned a great deal from him.

The professor said, "Yes, he was a very knowledgeable man, a walking library, he was always writing books, he spoke a number of languages, he was a famous man. He brought a lot of good things to the district. Those tangerine trees you have in your gardens, you're indebted to him for those. He brought those seeds all the way from Brazil."

"May he rest in peace," said the fishermen.

"There's a nice story about him concerning the mausoleum," said the professor. "You know the mausoleum, that pile of old stones outside Bodrum?"

"Yes," said the villagers, "Of course we know it."

"It was the tomb of King Mauselos, but the English took it and brought it to their museum. And the Fisherman wrote a letter to the queen of England. He said that this work had been created to stand under the blue skies of Bodrum, not under the foggy, rainy skies of London. Six months later he got a letter from the director of the museum, he said don't worry, the ceiling of the room where it stands has been painted blue."

"The English are so clever," said Yusuf, "but my grandfather said they were treacherous. He said they stabbed us in the back during World War I."

Thus began one of the endless arguments between those who praised English manufactured goods and those who felt the English were treacherous. None of the many young English tourists who came now were seen as a threat, though the villagers didn't like the way they shouted when they got drunk. During the day they surfed or swam, but in the evening they always drank until they were out of control. The bar owners loved them. The girls wore black lipstick and black fingernail polish. It was frightening to encounter them on a dark street at night.

The professor told them, "Don't forget, you're living on what was once one of the most important civilizations. You know the inscribed stones, marble, and mosaics you find when you dig a foundation, these are very valuable. Don't break them, cover them up, or use them as building materials, tell the authorities about them. Even Alexander the Great passed through here."

The fishermen looked at each other as if to ask, Who's Alexander the Great?

ustafa was accustomed to the heat, but on that August day he was dripping with sweat. Even in the prosecutor's ice-cold office there were beads of sweat on his brow, and he kept wiping it with his handkerchief, even though he realized that the prosecutor had noticed this. The prosecutor was saying that the survivors had seen a woman tie a baby into a small, inflatable boat, had he seen anything like this? At that moment Mustafa had great difficulty not saying yes. Perhaps it was best to tell the truth and give the baby up. Perhaps the woman in the hospital was the baby's real mother. If that was the case, he couldn't keep the poor woman's baby.

The prosecutor looked at the file and said that three refugees had been brought to the hospital. One of them, a woman who was thought to be Afghan, was still in a coma, and one of the men had mentioned a baby in his statement.

"He said that before the boat sank, he saw a young Afghan woman weeping as she put a baby in a little inflatable boat. The coast guard hasn't found a baby, alive or dead, or any inflatable boat. That's why I'm asking, did you at least see a small, red boat?"

Mustafa felt an overwhelming desire to say yes, indeed, he'd begun to say it but then he changed his mind. The baby had been in his house for days—how could he confess that he'd hidden the baby from the law? And if he did, it wasn't just himself, Mesude would be considered guilty as well. The baby didn't have a mother, and he didn't want him sent to an orphanage. No, no, he couldn't send that baby to an orphanage.

"No, sir," he said, "I didn't notice anything like that. I'll look more carefully the next time I go out."

He was very tense. He wiped the back of his neck with his handkerchief.

The prosecutor printed the statement, then Mustafa signed it and left. He was dripping with sweat, the sun was making him delirious, the shade had grown darker. He bought a soft drink, guzzled it down, and put the cold bottle on the back of his neck. It didn't help.

———

*I*n the evening, he and Mesude sat and had a whispered conversation about what they were going to do. The baby was sleeping peacefully in the cradle. The wind was rattling the windows.

"The south wind has begun," said Mustafa, "tomorrow the fish will act as if they're drunk."

Mesude ignored this and said, "Mustafa, there's no way out of this. We're breaking the law, we have to take care of it right away, this is no joke."

"What should we do?" asked Mustafa. He was falling apart and felt completely exhausted. He hadn't touched his tea. "What should we do?" he repeated.

"Do what I already told you to do, bring the baby out in the boat with you, bring him back, say you found him, and hand him over."

"The wind is going to be quite strong tomorrow." The windows were now rattling almost constantly; the kitchen window had been blown open.

"You're not listening to me."

"I am listening...but the wind..."

"I'm telling you to bring the baby back tomorrow."

He went into the kitchen to close the window. She followed him.

"Tomorrow."

"What about tomorrow?"

"You're going to give them the baby."

"No, that won't work. It will be obvious that the baby hasn't been floating in the sea for days, he's been fed, cleaned, and cared for. Should I leave the baby hungry again, dirty him, bring him back to the half-dead state he was in?"

Mesude paused and thought, then said, "You're right. When you first brought him, didn't I tell you to hand him over? Didn't I tell you this wouldn't work?"

Meanwhile, after a crackling of the microphone, the evening call to prayer echoed through the village. They fell silent. They didn't pray, but respecting the call to prayer was one of the unwritten rules of the village.

Because the days were so long in summer, the call to prayer came quite late. It was slowly beginning to grow dark. The evening crept into the village so slowly you didn't notice it until it was already dark. The warm wind from the sea rattled the makeshift windows.

"I'm starting to get a bad feeling," said Mesude. "Last night I dreamt there was a shark-faced man standing in the doorway. He was standing right there, looking at me."

"He had the face of a shark?"

"Yes. He had a human face with the mouth of a shark. He was going to do something bad."

"God forbid..."

"Yes, believe me, he was going to do something bad."

The south wind steadily grew more violent. It was like a horde of mounted warriors assaulting the shore. The bare lightbulb hanging over the patio swung back and forth. Patches of light and shadow moved from side to side.

The roaring of the wind gave Mustafa the feeling that something bad could happen at any moment. He felt embarrassed about the way he'd spoken to the prosecutor. He'd said he would look more carefully next time. Had he told him that if he found a baby in a boat he would bring it to him? He was so confused he couldn't remember what he'd said. Perhaps the police would come soon.

Mesude said, "For days I've had to find excuses to keep my mother from dropping by. Your mother is in Nazilli, but mine is here. How can I tell her not to come?"

Mustafa answered in an irritable manner, raising his voice. "Just be quiet for a while."

"Fine, if you're not going to listen to me, you figure it out on your own."

"The wind is going to get even stronger tonight. I hope the boats don't get piled on top of each other. I moored my boat well, but..."

"You're impossible. You either don't say anything at all, or you talk nonsense. I give up. You do whatever you want."

"I'm talking about the wind. About the boats. About our livelihood."

"Was that what we were talking about just now?"

"No, but it's still important. It's our livelihood."

Mesude took him by the chin and made him look at her.

"You're doing this to escape. That's what you always do when there's a problem you can't solve. You either go to sleep or escape."

"I'm not escaping."

"You are."

"I tell you I'm not."

"That's exactly what you're doing."

"Fine. Since I'm escaping, I'm going to go out."

She made a face and went inside. She was hurt. He went out, slammed the door behind him, and sat in the chair beneath the vines. Mustafa didn't sleep at all that night—he sat in the chair until morning. There were problems he had to solve. Before dawn he went down to the harbor and went out fishing. He continued to think while he was fishing; he made a plan. He approached a small island that was crawling with snakes; he stared at the rocks for a long time. The rocks reflected a host of colors, from bright green to purple and from purple to red. For a while there'd been a seal who had had its nest in these rocks, but he hadn't seen it for a long time.

Close to the waterline there were moray eels in the crevices. At night their heads would emerge from their nests. That day a lot of puffer fish and lionfish got caught in his net. He grumbled under his breath, put on his thick gloves, held the puffer fish carefully, cut off the tails he would be paid for, and then tossed the lionfish into the hold without touching their poisonous spines. *Let me bring some of these home this evening*, he thought, *Mesude likes them.* He regretted having behaved badly to her. *I guess this baby has got me all worked up.*

Every day, motor yachts that looked like giant irons would pass him. The fishing boats would be tossed about in their wakes. Every year these yachts got bigger—they were now seventy to eighty meters long. They churned up the sea as they sliced through it. Mustafa had grown accustomed to them, but that day they annoyed him. He stood and shouted at one of them.

On his return he scanned the blue water. Oh, if he could only see a small inflatable boat. With a baby in it. Sunburned and hungry, but alive. He would take it straight to the prosecutor. Of course that wasn't going to happen. What was he going to do? In fact there was a plan forming in his mind, but how was he going to explain it to Mesude?

When he arrived home with a bag of lionfish, he saw the baby in his mother-in-law's lap. Raziye Hanım looked quite young for her age. She was singing the baby a lullaby. Mesude took after her mother—they both had green eyes and the proud stance of Cretan women. No one would deny that they were the most beautiful women in the village. In this sandy-haired woman's arms, the baby looked very dark. His skin color was different, more olive, and there was no re-semblance at all.

When Raziye Hanım was eighteen, she was married to the son of a man her father admired, a car dealer—*A good family, a very good family, and they're wealthy too*, he would say—and moved to the town. When the young man went to a village restaurant once with his friends, he'd seen Raziye and been smitten by her. Even though he seemed to be as hardworking as his father, Raziye realized a few months after the wedding that he was a complete rake; he spent his life drinking in nightclubs and chasing after women. After satisfying his lust for her for a few months, he returned to his old ways. When he came home drunk toward morning and she asked him where he'd been, he would say she had no right to ask him that. Later he started saying, "That's just how I am, I'm a man." Later still things started to get quite ugly. Even from the start it was not a marriage of love, but the sympathy and respect she felt for him due to his intense interest in her soon vanished. Finally, she realized it wasn't going to work, so she packed her bags and returned to her mother's house.

Her mother was an empathetic woman; she understood the situation. But her father wasn't like that. As Raziye would say, he was old-fashioned. He wouldn't allow her back in the house. "A married woman's place is by her husband's side. There's no place for you in this house," he said. Her mother was upset, but she couldn't get past his stern nature. Raziye's husband came to get her, and she returned to the town. The man was running after other women, so why was he so insistent on keeping her in his house? They weren't really living together anyway, so why should she sit home alone waiting for him? In the end she became so unhappy that she made the decision to leave him no matter what. If she had to, she could live with her aunt, but just at this point she realized she was pregnant. She wasn't too concerned when she was late—after all. her periods were irregular—but when a month passed she went to see a doctor at the public hospital. There was also a slight discharge. If she'd been in the village she would have resorted to folk remedies, but now she had no choice but to tell the doctor. She'd never been to a doctor before. When the doctor gave her an ultrasound and spread her legs with a strange device, she almost died of mortification. Even though the doctor was a woman she couldn't look her in the face.

Now she understood why Caner wanted to keep her in his house. The man was going to continue his life of drinking and womanizing while his wife waited at home and produced children. Raziye was deeply shaken. She hated the man so intensely that hearing him stumble in at night made her want to vomit. She regarded the new life beginning to form within her with a mixture of delight and horror. She both wanted and didn't want the baby. This baby might tie Raziye to the man she hated for the rest of her life. The very thought made her ill. Then early one morning she received the news that was a disaster for everyone else but salvation for her, news that was front-page news in the local paper and provided endless gossip for the men in the coffeehouses and the women whispering at home—*God knows, she wasn't even the slightest bit upset.* When the doorbell rang that night, Raziye knew that something had happened. She opened the door with the foreboding that someone was either in the hospital or dead. When she saw two policemen whose faces were shaded by their peaked hats, she knew that it was serious: her heart raced as she asked them what had happened. The policemen hesitated when they saw she was pregnant, then told her that her husband was in the hospital. There was an accident, they said, and he had been taken to the hospital.

At that moment Raziye knew that her life had changed irrevocably, and despite the sense of guilt that suddenly rose within her, asked hopefully, "Is he dead?" The policemen hesitated, then one of them said, "Not quite...He's injured...it's kind of serious." She understood the situation. She went to get a sweater, and went with them to the hospital.

Caner had left a bar with a woman late at night, got into his white car, drove out along the dirt road toward the point, then somehow managed to drive over a cliff. His blood alcohol level was reported to be high. Some villagers had heard the crash and called the police. The woman was badly injured. In her statement she had said that she and Caner were heading to a hotel outside town but that Caner had been very drunk and lost control of the car on a curve; she didn't remember anything after that. Caner had died in the ambulance. The doctors were solicitous when they told her this, kept touching her shoulder as if they were trying to comfort her, kept asking her if she needed anything, trying as they did so to conceal the pity they felt for a young pregnant woman whose husband had died while fooling around with another woman. They were amazed at her fortitude, at how she didn't shed a single tear as she listened to the details.

Raziye returned to her father's house the next day. Of course he couldn't object under the circumstances. She refused to accept her inheritance from the man she hated. She gave birth to her daughter as an aggrieved widow who had gained everyone's sympathy. Her liberation from Caner seemed like divine justice. God had heard her. This accident seemed like a miracle. Raziye became a religious woman after that. She never failed to pray or fast. Though until then, like many of the younger people in the village, she hadn't thought much about religion. Raziye's father had died when Mesude was still a baby, and her mother died two years later. She tried to raise her daughter to be a religious person. But it turned out that it was in Mesude's nature to rebel against any rules or pressure, including those of religion. Her attitude was one of *I'll listen to you, but I'll make up my own mind.* After that point, nobody could reach the girl. This attitude reminded Raziye of how Caner used to say, "That's just the way I am." Her daughter must have inherited this side of her personality from her father.

She didn't push it, because she knew Mesude had a stronger moral compass than anyone. When she turned eighteen, she made her decision to marry

Mustafa, and her mother didn't interfere. She thought that perhaps her daughter had done the right thing. She remembered the decision her father had made for her and thought that perhaps marrying for love was better.

Mustafa was two years older than Mesude. They'd spent their childhood together in the village. They played leapfrog, swam, played football in front of Gırdinni's coffeehouse, helped the fishermen mend nets, washed out the boats, went fishing, wrestled. When they were little, there was no distinction between boys and girls, but after puberty, when hormones began to flow through their veins, there was a strange awkwardness between the boys and girls.

Mesude didn't know when it happened, when it started, but she became modest about her body, she didn't go swimming with boys anymore, she didn't wrestle with them either. The change wasn't sudden, from one day to the next. The hormones took their time seizing control of their minds and bodies.

One day Mesude noticed how handsome Mustafa was—she'd never noticed this before. *What nice eyes he has*, she thought. There was a strange bashfulness and awkwardness between Mesude and Mustafa.

When they saw each other, they felt uncomfortable, and kept avoiding each other's glances. They'd lost the easy balance they'd had. Once, when she was looking out to sea, she turned her head suddenly and saw that Mustafa was watching her. In her budding womanhood it pleased her to be admired. Then she began to think about Mustafa day and night. She would sit by the window that overlooked the harbor and watch the boat he was in until it disappeared.

Raziye noticed the state her daughter was in and jokingly asked, "What's the matter with you these days, are you in love?" Mesude answered sharply, "Mother, don't talk nonsense." Then one day Mustafa came up to her and, blushing, managed to say, "It's been a long time since we went fishing. If you like, I can borrow my master's boat on Sunday and we can go fishing together."

Mesude was surprised. Her first thought was to say no, but the words "We'll see" came out of her mouth. "If there's nothing else I have to do I might go."

Mustafa was pleased, as if his life had depended on this maybe. He'd become aware of her quite suddenly. One evening, when they were sitting around a fire roasting quail with a group of friends, he found it difficult to look at Mesude. She was sitting next to him, and when his hand accidentally touched hers he immediately pulled it away. He felt his cheeks burning. The vague, timid transition from friendship to love, the hesitation, *did I go too far or was I too timid*, the struggle to find meaning in every word or glance, feeling like a fisherman lost at sea, trying to find his way.

On Sunday Mustafa went to the boat early and got everything ready. Will she come, will she not come, will she come, will she not come...He kept glancing up to the top of the hill. Then he saw her coming down the dirt road, walking as if she were gliding. He felt a sense of panic. As they moved out to sea they spoke about fish, fishing lines, and the wind. Mustafa was unable to bring himself to move the conversation into dangerous territory. But as they were heading back, fearing he might not get another chance, he asked the question that had been on his mind since the night before. He pointed to a pod of dolphins leaping past in the distance and asked, "How do the males and the females find each other in the vast ocean, how do they find their mates? Do they fall in love too?"

The girl suddenly became alert. She said, "I don't know," then fell silent. He didn't say anything else either. Then a while later he said, "I think they do. I think they fall in love the way we do. That's how it seems to me, but what do I know?"

They both suddenly rose to their feet, rocking the boat. Mustafa managed to say, "Mesude, please forgive me, but I'm in love with you." Then he jumped into the sea. Mesude smiled.

Hesude greeted her husband in a somewhat petulant manner, took the fish, and went into the kitchen.

Raziye Hanım said, "He's a beautiful baby, but what are we going to do with him, he's going to grow, he's going to get sick, he's going to need to go to school. We won't be able to hide him, Mustafa."

"You're right," said Mustafa in a soft tone. "I brought fish; stay for dinner so we can talk this over. We're confused too. But first I need a drink."

She smiled. She liked Mustafa, but because she was religious she didn't like that he drank, at least in her presence. But that evening was special—she could see how overwhelmed he was—so she didn't say anything. They sat at a small, square table under the vine on the patio. The heat of the day had diminished, and a refreshing breeze was blowing from the sea. The scent of jasmine almost clung to their skin. Mesude had her own method of frying fish. She would heat oil in two pans and cook the fish first in one and then the other. This way the fish absorbed less oil. The white flesh of the lionfish was delicious.

Mustafa kept giving Mesude tender glances, but she wasn't responding. He thanked Mesude for the delicious meal and raised his glass. Raziye looked away and muttered something under her breath.

In the twilight Mustafa said, "The world is full of wonders. These fish left the Red Sea and came to the Aegean, then ended up on our table. Fate. God destined for them to come here." The two women knew where he was going with this. But still, Raziye Hamım said, "Don't mention God's name with rakı in your mouth."

Then she said, "Mustafa, look, I've warmed to the baby too, he's an innocent child, we're migrants too, our grandparents had to leave Crete and come all the way here, they called us unbelievers, they called us migrants, they didn't accept us but we hung on, we understand these people's plight. I wish there was some way we could look after this innocent baby, some way we could raise him, but there isn't. They'll throw us all in jail."

In a reproachful tone, Mesude said, "I've been saying the same thing, but I can't get through to him."

"You're both absolutely right. There's nothing I can say. Every time I decide we should give him up, I look at his sleeping face, or the way he drinks milk, and it kills me. They'll send him to an orphanage, who knows what will happen to him there."

They sat in silence for a time. The three of them were lost in thought. Then Mustafa decided it was time to tell them about the plan that had been rattling around his mind for days.

"Something occurred to me. You know Filiz is pregnant, she'll be giving birth any day now, if she hasn't already."

Mesude looked at him in bewilderment. "So, that's wonderful for Filiz, but what does it have to do with our situation?"

Mustafa's younger sister was about to give birth in Nazilli. His mother was with her. The plan that Mustafa had been working out in his mind for the past few days relied on this. They would take the baby to Nazilli, stay there for a time, then come back with the baby. They'd tell everyone that Filiz had given birth to twins, that she felt she couldn't manage two babies, and she'd given one to them. After all, they'd lost their own child. The entire family had been devastated by this. And this way they could avoid any suspicions aroused by the baby's dark skin. His brother-in-law wasn't very dark-skinned, but no one in these parts knew him. They could say that he took after his father.

Mesude and her mother listened in amazement. They shook their heads as if to say no, that can't possibly work, but Mustafa spoke with such conviction he was practically begging them, and they began to wonder if it might work. It was true that nobody in the village had any connections in Nazilli. It was far away in another province, and they'd only seen Filiz's husband at the wedding. They wouldn't recognize him if they saw him. If Filiz agreed to the plan then there was no obstacle. He didn't know how they would handle hospital records, but this way they could get Deniz registered. Then all their troubles would be over. If they stayed in Nazilli for a month, it wouldn't matter that their baby was a couple of weeks older. Mustafa had been working on the plan for days; he'd worked out all the details.

Raziye listened to him carefully, then said, "Fine, but what is your sister going to say about this? And more important, what is her husband going to say?" This was the question that had been bothering Mustafa. Filiz didn't know about the migrants who'd been found, or about the baby. Perhaps she would agree because she loved her older brother, but how would they convince her husband? He was under no obligation to register the baby as his own.

Mustafa was also counting on their mother, Melahat. Filiz was deeply attached to her mother. Even though she was a married woman, the two of them were inseparable. That's why she'd spent the last months in Nazilli with her daughter and her husband. He hoped his mother wouldn't disappoint him.

His mother-in-law said, "What can I say, Mustafa. You've already made up your mind, I just hope it works out." After she left, Mustafa and Mesude began making travel plans. They had to take a local bus to the town, then from there take an intercity bus to Nazilli, but this was impossible. The intercity bus wouldn't be a problem, but they couldn't board the local bus with the baby.

Night was falling on the village, and even the tourists had disappeared. The sea was calm.

The fisherman went to the closet, retrieved the money he'd hidden there for emergencies, and put it in his pocket. They'd go through all of it on this trip. However things worked out, he wasn't going to have any income for a while. When people saw the exorbitant prices restaurants charged for fish, they thought fishermen made a lot of money. But fishermen had expenses such as fuel, nets, and paint, and lived from hand to mouth.

Mesude dressed the baby and packed a suitcase. They put the baby in the basket and covered him, and Mustafa took the suitcase. It was almost morning, and they didn't meet anyone as they made their way down the dirt road. The fishing harbor was deserted as well. Mesude and the baby boarded the boat, then Mustafa untied the ropes and jumped aboard. He didn't start the motor, but instead rowed out of the harbor. They moved out to sea without anyone noticing them. Out on the water there was a refreshing coolness, and stars shone like gems in the sky.

If his friends didn't see his boat in the harbor or at sea, they would worry and inform the coast guard. In an hour or so he was going to send a text message to Yusuf saying they'd gone to his sister's because she was giving birth. He'd also invented a reason why his boat was missing. After rowing for quite some time, Mustafa started the motor. Then he sped through the darkness across the waters he knew so well. He was going to leave the boat with his close friend Süleyman in a fishing harbor near the town.

Everything went according to plan. They passed the town and entered a small fishing harbor. Mustafa tied his boat to Süleyman's, a blue-and-red fishing boat named *Mermaid*, then sent him a text message. *Sorry, my friend, but some work came up for me in the area and I have to leave my boat here for a while.* They began walking toward town and reached the bus terminal just as dawn was breaking. Mustafa bought two tickets for the Denizli bus, saying they would get off at Nazilli. Then they sat and waited on the white plastic chairs in the waiting room. Mustafa got some sesame rings, right out of the oven, from the bakery, and the tea boy brought them freshly brewed tea. The sesame rings were hot and crunchy. After their second tea they felt restored. Mesude changed the baby on a plastic chair and then fed him. Then they dozed in their seats as they waited for the bus.

Thankfully everything had gone well so far. Strangely, the fisherman felt both calm and anxious. From time to time there was a twinkle in his eye as he smiled, and then he would suddenly become serious again. As if a shadow was passing across his face. The baby was in his arms, and Mesude was sleeping on his shoulder. They were both calm.

Later in the morning it became more crowded. First the tradesmen began appearing, then locals on motor scooters, bus passengers. The grocery stores, greengrocers, fishmongers, souvenir shops, and money changers began to open. The normal life of the town had begun. The foreign tourists never appeared before noon. The rising sun announced the fierce heat that would come. Just then they heard the announcement that their bus was leaving. They were the first to board, and their seats were in the front. The bus was half-full. Fortunately they hadn't seen anyone they knew.

They slept most of the way to Nazilli. At one point Mustafa woke up and stared at the baby in his arms. *No, whatever happens I'm not going to give him up*, he thought. This baby was a gift from father dolphin.

Nazilli is a small town. It wasn't a touristy town on the seaside, so it hadn't been developed as much as their district. They had no trouble finding the house.

The giant fish was now pulling the boat, making it fly through the water. Nothing could stop this hero of the open sea. The fisherman was no match for it. It could keep dragging the boat forever. Mustafa's hands were in shreds from holding the line for days, pulling it in when he could and letting it out when he had to. Suddenly the fish jumped, rising like a dark-blue tower from the sea. Its sword reached toward the sky. As soon as he saw it, Mustafa murmured, *My God, what a beautiful beast you created. How could I not spare such a magnificent creature? Farewell, fish.* Then he grabbed his knife and cut the line. The line quickly disappeared into the deep sea. Mustafa felt a great sense of relief. *There's no other path than fate. That means it wasn't his time. Farewell, fish, you deserve to live more than any of us.*

———

He woke with a sense of happiness. At first everything seemed strange in the darkness; it took him a few seconds to grasp where he was. It comforted him to see Mesude lying next to him. They were at Filiz's house. Because they'd arrived with a baby, they'd had to tell the whole story as soon as they arrived. Filiz would be giving birth soon; she was having difficulty walking. She and her mother were astounded by what Mustafa told them. They didn't know what to say. Mustafa told them his plan in a pleading manner. "That's our situation, there's no other way." Mesude didn't say anything at all.

Filiz said, "How is this possibly going to work? I leave the hospital with one baby and then say I have two? How is it going to be possible to register your baby? And how are we going to explain all of this to Selim? I've never heard of anything like this."

Selim was at the bank; he would come when his shift was over. He knew that Mustafa and Mesude were coming, but he had no idea about the baby.

Their mother said, "Let's stop for a moment, have something to eat, think things through calmly, but of course the most important thing is what Selim is going to say."

"Are we just going to tell the man he suddenly has another child? Even if Selim says yes, how is the registration at the hospital going to be handled? There are rules and regulations in this country." Filiz's cheeks had turned a deep red.

In a faint voice, Mustafa said, "You can give birth at home, with a midwife, the way all of us were born."

Filiz looked at him in amazement and rose to her feet. "God give me patience, this is unbelievable." With that she left the room.

Their mother said, "Son, there's no way, she can't give birth at home. She's had a difficult pregnancy, God forbid something should go wrong... No, no, forget about it."

Mesude turned to her husband and said, "Why don't we rest a little and then go back home."

"No, let's just think a little. Meanwhile let's go set the table."

Mesude was offended when Filiz said she wasn't feeling well and stayed in her room all afternoon. "Look, she doesn't want us here, let's just leave. There's no reason for us to stay where we're not wanted."

Mustafa understood how she felt. Filiz's behavior had hurt him too, but he didn't want to give up on the plan. "Hold on, all of this came out of the blue for her, and she's pregnant, she's emotional."

"As if she's the only one who's ever been pregnant. We've all been there, there's no excuse for driving guests out of your house, she's putting on airs because her husband is a banker, she looks down on us."

No matter what Mustafa said, he couldn't get through to her; she was insisting they find a place to stay.

"We can find a bed-and-breakfast like the one Aunt Fatma runs."

It was almost evening; how were they going to find a place? Were there in fact any bed-and-breakfasts in Nazilli? A hotel would be too expensive. What was wrong with waiting until morning? But Mesude was determined. Mustafa realized that her mind was made up, so he picked up the suitcase and they left the room.

His mother was knitting in the living room. "Where are you going?" she asked, and Mustafa told her what was going on. She stood and blocked their way. "I won't allow it, you're not going anywhere." She snatched the bag from Mustafa, took Mesude by the arm, and sat her on the sofa. "Look, don't pay any attention to Filiz, she's had a difficult pregnancy, she already had two miscarriages. This time she couldn't get out of bed for three months, she cries all the time, her nerves are shot. It doesn't have anything to do with you, believe me."

She spoke in such a strong and decisive manner that no one could object. Mustafa brought the suitcase to their room, and when he returned his mother was playing with the baby. He asked where Mesude was. She nodded toward Filiz's room.

When Mesude entered the fancily furnished room, she saw Filiz crying silently on the bed. When she saw Mesude she sat up. "Come on in. Please excuse me, I was rude to you, my nerves are really shot." She lowered her voice and continued. "I've already had two miscarriages—there's no telling what will happen with this one. I haven't told Selim yet, but the other day the doctors said there's a chance the baby might come out backward. They're talking about a cesarean, and I'm scared."

Mesude sat next to her, put her arm around her, and wiped away her tears. "I understand you, Filiz, I've known you since you were a little girl. Mustafa was thoughtless to dump this problem at your feet in such difficult times. It's best if we leave, don't take it the wrong way, it's not because of you."

"Please don't go. I've been lying here trying to think of how to get you to forgive me." When Mesude insisted, she began crying even more. "I'll never be able to forgive myself. If you leave it will be much worse. Be the bigger person. Please don't go."

When Mesude saw that she really was in a bad state, she said, "Fine, we'll stay a day or two."

"In fact seeing you here has been good for me, you're like a letter from home." Then, in tears, she began unburdening herself. "I feel like I'm suffocating here. I miss our village so much, I miss the sea, the wind, the smell, the meadows, and the mountains, I miss them so much." As she spoke she calmed down a bit and began wiping away her tears. "Selim is a good man, but he's so boring. He goes to the bank every morning and comes home in the evening. Sometimes he comes home for lunch, but then it's back to the bank. There are a few other banker's wives I socialize with, but I'm used to going fishing, casting nets, gathering herbs and mushrooms in the mountains. I feel as if I'm in a dungeon—seeing you made me realize how unhappy I am here. Thankfully my dear mother is here to support me. If not for her I would have gone out of my mind by now."

When Mesude put herself in the girl's place, she understood completely. If, God forbid, she should have to leave behind her garden and the honeysuckles, jasmine, banana trees, lavender, tangerine trees and lemon trees, the vine that produced juicy, seedless grapes, the pergola, the chickens that gave her eggs every morning, the sea breezes, the north wind, the great variety of fresh fish, and move to an apartment on the second floor of this dim, cabbage-smelling, five-story building with shoes piled in front of the doors, it would drive her out of her mind.

*L*ook, when you take that baby in your arms, all of that will be behind you. You'll be happy, yes, the place you're used to is important, but your home and your family are here. You'll get used to it in time." She reached out, touched Filiz's hair, and continued. "The city housewives who come to our village don't like it there. They say it's too damp, even the walls are rotting, everyone has rheumatism, the old people are all bent double. They see earning your living from the sea as difficult and dangerous. Isn't it better to get a salary every month? There are no bars or discos on the shore, it's harder to keep the children under control, there's all kinds of immorality. They also complain about how expensive it is. They inflate the prices because of the tourists."

"It's true, life is less expensive here."

"Everything has its good side and its bad side. Look, do you know if it's going to be a boy or a girl? Have you decided on a name yet?"

"It's a boy. Selim wanted to name him Hamit after his father, but I want a more modern name. I want to name him Keremcan."

ore than sixteen thousand migrants have lost their lives in the Mediterranean."

At another time they may not have paid much attention to this news, but now they gave their full attention to the young woman who was presenting this story. They might have glanced at the television in passing, but now it caused them genuine distress to see the footage of inflatable boats crammed with migrants. Because one of them was sleeping in the room with them. They didn't know what had happened to the baby's parents. They'd most probably drowned.

The Turkish authorities who were being interviewed placed the blame on Greece. They said the Greek coast guard were sinking the inflatable boats and leaving the migrants to their deaths. The Greek side insisted this was slander, that the Turks weren't stopping the refugees, that they were sending them to Greece. They said there were forty thousand refugees being housed on five islands.

Later an official from the United Nations was interviewed. He spoke of the terrible conditions in the camps, children being bitten by rats, women giving birth on dirt floors, inadequate toilets and washing facilities. The footage of the camps was disturbing. As Mustafa and Mesude watched together, they both thought the same thing: *It's a good thing the baby isn't in one of those camps.* The very thought shook them to the core. As they watched the news while drinking their coffee after dinner, the entire family was horrified. Selim said, "Sixteen thousand lives have been lost; it's difficult to even begin to grasp that." Melahat put down her knitting and said, "What are they fleeing that makes them willing to risk their lives like this? Who would take little children on such a dangerous journey?"

Selim was a calm, soft man. When he returned from the bank, he'd greeted his guests politely. He was a plump, balding man of medium height. His cheeks were pink. He was a kind, courteous man with a soft voice and demeanor. The distressing footage continued, and Melahat signaled to Selim to change the channel, pointing at Filiz. Selim immediately said, "Excuse me, but I'm changing the channel."

That night, Mesude asked, "Selim is a good man, isn't he? He's certainly very polite."

It was a double bed, but it was narrow, and it also creaked. Mustafa slept with two pillows, but Mesude slept with a single pillow. Even though the curtains were closed, light from the streetlamp still streamed in.

"Yes. I've only met him a few times and we've never really talked, but he really is a good man."

"I suppose he's going to help us. At least that's how it seemed to me."

"That's how it seemed to me too. He was very understanding."

"And it's good that Filiz had her tantrum."

"Why?"

"She felt really bad afterward. She'll be more reasonable now."

"Good. Let's go to sleep then."

Mesude sat up and leaned on her elbow. "You know, there was no need for any of this." There was reproach in her voice.

"How so?"

"We could have had our own baby. Couldn't I have given birth? I'm still young. Then we wouldn't have been obliged to anyone. But you said no."

Mustafa sat up too. "We almost lost you when Deniz was born. Didn't the doctor keep saying that you couldn't get pregnant again?"

"But I wasn't your primary concern. You said you couldn't replace Deniz with another child. You kept saying you didn't want another child. Isn't that true, wasn't that the real reason?"

"Yes, but I changed my mind later. I changed my mind about it being unfair to the child to bring it into the world."

"So why didn't you tell me? Why did we use birth control?"

"Later on I worried about your illness. I was afraid of losing you."

"Don't say illness. I'm not sick."

"Of course not."

"I'm at least as much of a woman as Filiz."

"Yes, of course you are, but the doctor…"

"The doctor said it could be dangerous, she didn't say it was definitely dangerous. We could have consulted another doctor."

Mustafa didn't say anything. She studied his face in the dim light. "Why aren't you saying anything?"

"The blood," said Mustafa. "There was so much blood."

"Anyway, I survived, and so did our baby."

*T*hey fell silent. Neither of them wanted to admit they were thinking about how their child hadn't survived for long. There was nothing to say. The reluctance to see the pain in each other's eyes remained suspended between them, and distanced them from each other.

*S*ometime later Mustafa said, "Fine, the past is the past. I didn't go looking for this baby. God gave him to me."

"When you were fishing."

"When I was fishing. A dolphin brought him."

"I wonder where his mother is, whether she's alive or dead."

"Let's go to sleep," he said as he put his arms around her. She kissed him on the lips. It was clear she wanted to make love. They made love briefly but fiercely. Mustafa pulled away; Mesude tried to hold him but she wasn't strong enough. Then she felt hurt. She turned her back to him and wept silently.

Water boiling in the kitchen, towels and cloths, women rushing in and out of the room and the sound of moaning that pierced Mustafa through and through, Mesude's screams, *Something's wrong, I can feel it*, stopping his mother-in-law, taking her hands and asking, *What's going on, what's going on*, the serious look on her face as she said *Hold on*, how difficult it was to wait, the midwife emerging covered in sweat and blood, an old woman in the kitchen crushing herbs and seeds with a mortar and pestle to make a healing balm, spreading it on gauze and bringing it into the room, nobody would answer his questions, meanwhile Ömer was running around outside shouting that Mesude was dead, his mother telling him to go to the coffeehouse, he had no business being in the house, thinking that he wouldn't be able to live if Mesude died, not being able to even conceive of life without her, his mother emerging from the room with a baby in her arms, *You have a son*, then that terrifying silence, the ominous silence after all the screaming, not a sound coming from the room, even Ömer had stopped shouting, Mustafa racing into the room without glancing at the baby, blood everywhere, as if Mesude were lying on a red flag, the fear and horror, the blood was so very red, it glistened, Mesude's weak smile, the smell of birthwort and cloves. Then holding the baby, the baby's smell combined with that of the birthwort. The unbelievable joy and surprise of holding their baby.

A few days later Raziye brought her pale daughter to the public hospital. Mesude was given the same embarrassing examination she'd had when she was young. Afterward the doctor said with a serious expression, *Your daughter is lucky to be alive, she really should have given birth in the hospital, I don't know how the midwife stopped the bleeding, your daughter survived by coincidence, but it's too risky for her to ever get pregnant again. In her position I wouldn't.*

Mesude looked at the woman doctor, who was much older, and thought, *You couldn't anyway.* She didn't like the woman's manner and the way she spoke. She herself thought she might have been at greater risk in the hospital. Zübeyde the midwife had helped all the women in the village give birth. She knew all the medicinal herbs and seeds; she eased the fevers and chased off the demons that plague new mothers.

*O*n the day Deniz disappeared into the vast, dark sea she remembered that birth. Indeed, she'd never forgotten it.

*T*heir hosts apologized and insisted sincerely that they stay, so Mustafa and Mesude changed their minds about leaving. Mesude and her mother-in-law took over the kitchen. They wouldn't let Filiz lift a finger. Mustafa started taking long walks through the city after dinner. He walked and walked through empty streets in the cold light of the streetlamps, flanked on both sides by identical concrete apartment buildings. Everyone was inside watching television; it was deserted except for the cats, and the street dogs, from which he kept his distance.

Mustafa had never been this far from the sea. The colors and sounds and smells were different; he didn't understand how people could live inland. He wouldn't live in that place for all the money in the world. He often felt sorry for Filiz. His sister was a child of the sea as well—when she was still just five or six she used to catch crabs on the shore and toss them into her little blue plastic bucket. Later she got quite good at fishing. She would cast nets, prepare reels, and put out the trotline—she had a good relationship with the sea. Indeed sometimes she showed herself to be even better at fishing than Mesude. At times he'd been amazed at her expertise in catching large fish.

The merciless game between fisherman and fish was an important part of this. If the line was too loose, the fish would turn, bite the line, and free itself. It could also wriggle free if the line was too taut. It took considerable mastery to know when to let the line out and when to pull it in. Filiz was one of the best at this.

Living in this place must have been difficult for her. He could see that she felt as if she were drowning. Sea people should stay by the sea, and inland people should stay inland.

Yusuf called when they'd been there six or seven days. Another body had wound up in the Stutterer's net. He'd been excited because he thought he'd caught a large fish, but it turned out to be the body of a man. Mustafa sighed. It was bad enough they had to deal with lionfish, puffer fish, and fish farms, but now there were dead bodies everywhere.

No one knew how many bodies were eaten by fish. And in turn they would eat those fish. It made him ill to think about this. It made him more ill when Yusuf said everyone was wondering about his absence. "The police asked about you too. I told them I didn't know anything about it, but they said word was going around the village that you had a baby. They say you're hiding a baby in your house, you know what the village is like and how people love to gossip, but I think you should get back here as soon as possible."

When he told Mesude, who already had a lot on her mind, she didn't take it well. "This is all we need. How could anyone have seen him, how did word get out?" He hesitantly suggested that it might have been her mother, and she said, "Nonsense, she would never do that!"

"You're right, she wouldn't. But then who saw or heard the baby, those friends who came over for tea that day, do you think they might have suspected?" She thought a moment, then said, "Well, Ebru likes to gossip, I trust Aslı but I don't trust Ebru, I told her the sound she heard was a cat. but I suppose she didn't buy that."

"Well, we're going to bring the baby out into the open anyway. My brother-in-law is a very kind man."

*T*wo days later Filiz gave birth to a son in the hospital. Her doctor decided on a cesarean at the last moment. Everything went without a hitch. The baby was beautiful and healthy. When they brought him home he was wrapped in a frilly blue blanket and placed in the cradle. Relatives and neighbors said prayers for the baby. The new baby was just over seven pounds. Their own thin baby had managed to almost reach this weight. He wouldn't arouse suspicion because he was so small, but they still made sure no one saw the two babies together. One of the babies was pink and the other was quite dark—no one would believe they were twins. Mesude tried to think of a solution. In some villages there were Turks of African origin. No one knew where they'd come from, but at some point they'd settled there. They were called Arabs, but it was clear their ancestors had come from

Africa. The young girls rubbed yogurt on their faces to lighten their skin. And it worked. She would rub yogurt on the baby's face every day to whiten it. He wasn't that dark; his skin had more of an olive color.

One morning Mustafa and Mesude set out, got the boat from the fishing harbor near the town, and returned to their village. It was dark by the time they moored the boat; they didn't see anyone they knew. When they got home they found a note on the door; a summons from the prosecutor had been left with the mayor. They were uneasy throughout the night. Mustafa couldn't sleep, so he went to smoke a cigarette under the vine. There was no one in sight, just a few faintly lit boats that had gone out for shrimp. The village was asleep. People were harmless when they were asleep, but awake they were no different from the devil. People were always out to get each other; they always talked about the people they knew. Especially in a small place like this, where everyone behaved as if they were friends. The night smelled of jasmine and honeysuckle. This was a combination of smells he'd found intoxicating since childhood. He loved these smells and the smell of the sea. The smell of wet nets and the smell of the boat when it was wet with dew.

There was another smell he'd been trying for years to forget. The smell he got when he smelled the baby's neck. He'd tried for years to remember that smell, and now he was thankful that he could smell it again. *The way Deniz chuckled when I blew on him, the way he struggled to clap his hands, the way he squinted slightly as he watched his hands, the sounds he made as he kicked his legs in the air.*

He stubbed out his cigarette and tiptoed back inside.

Mesude said, "I'm not asleep, I'm going to get up and feed the baby." The baby made some faint moaning noises and then was quiet again. When Mustafa looked at that tiny baby, he was amazed at how he had survived so long in the dark on the open sea.

Mesude had left the lights off so as not to fully wake the baby. After she prepared the milk she left the light on in the kitchen. In the half darkness Mustafa saw that the baby's face was white. Mesude whispered, "I rubbed yogurt on his face."

The next morning, as Mustafa, with only two hours of sleep, a pounding headache, and a host of worries, was boarding the bus to go see the prosecutor, the villagers saw Mesude wheeling a baby carriage along the bumpy streets toward her mother's house. News like this woke ancient local traditions, and it spread through the village at a speed faster than that of the internet. Those who heard the news that *Mesude has a baby* all found excuses to go outside and stroll toward Raziye's house. Women gathered in groups of three or four and began talking. *So it's true that they took the baby they saved from the sunken boat, so this talk of a baby wasn't just empty gossip.* But if Mustafa had rescued the baby and hidden it as they said, why were they bringing the baby out into the open now? When they saw her emerge from her mother's house with the blue baby carriage in which she'd proudly strolled with the first Deniz, and which she'd kept in a corner with all the other things she hadn't been able to bring herself to give away even though they broke her heart every time she saw them, the village was abuzz. Women came over to say hello to Mesude. They leaned down to try to look at the baby. They could barely see his face because he was wrapped in muslin.

"We went to Nazilli to see my sister-in-law Filiz," Mesude told them. "She was pregnant, we went for the birth, she gave birth to twins, they gave one of them to us to raise. We decided together to name him Deniz."

Some of the women were touched by this and tearfully wished her the best.

They'd taken the first step. Deniz had been intro-
duced to the people of the village. But there were some
people who couldn't stop repeating that there was
something suspicious about the whole thing. There
were several bitter old women who thought it strange
that there were two stories about the baby. "The truth
will come out sooner or later," they said.

Mesude arrived home with her heart beating. She
closed the door tightly and fed the baby. She
couldn't get enough of watching him suck the bottle.
After she'd fed and changed Deniz, she wiped off the
talcum powder she'd put on his face to whiten it. She'd
used that as a stopgap, but there was something else
she was going to try. She'd seen a segment on television about how women in the Far East use rice water
to whiten their skin. In fact she quite liked his olive
skin, black eyes, and curly black eyelashes. But no one
would believe he was the fair-skinned Filiz's son.

eanwhile, Mustafa was sweating in front of the prosecutor. He'd been frightened when the prosecutor frowned and regarded him with a serious expression, but he was even more frightened by his stern tone. "Well, in her statement the refugee woman who has emerged from her coma claims to be the baby's mother. Her name," he paused to look at the file, "is Zilha Sherif. And the baby's name is"—again he paused to look at the file—"Samir Sherif. I've called you in to make an additional statement. You have to have seen something."

"I swear, sir, I've told you everything I know." Mustafa was in such a rush to defend himself that the prosecutor became even more suspicious. Indeed it had been Mustafa's nervousness that had given him away. The other fishermen had made their statements calmly, but Mustafa kept blushing and stuttering, and tried too hard to convince the prosecutor.

"So, what about the baby you have at home?"

Mustafa felt as if he'd been punched in the stomach. So, that story had reached the prosecutor. *Of course in a small place like this everyone knows everything.* Once again he was sweating in that cold office. Though in fact the office wasn't as cold as it had been before. Meanwhile the prosecutor was blowing his nose. *It was so cold in here it made him sick, he had to turn the air conditioner down.* His next thought was, *I'm an idiot, I'm such an idiot.*

"My sister gave birth to twins. She gave one of them to us, that's all there is to it." He couldn't think of anything else to say. When the prosecutor sneezed it didn't even occur to him to say "Bless you."

"What about his birth certificate and . . . achoo."

"Bless you."

"Enough of that. We're going to show the baby to its mother. Where did you say your sister lived? Nazilli. Her last name? Kumbasar." He turned to his assistant. "Look up the hospital records for Filiz Kumbasar in Nazilli."

Mustafa didn't even hear the rest. His head was spinning, and he felt as if he might fall to the floor at any moment. He didn't remember leaving the office or getting on the bus, he didn't know how he got home.

All he could say when his wife asked him in alarm if anything was wrong was "We're ruined." Then he went to bed and fell into a restless sleep. Whenever Mustafa faced disaster and couldn't think of a solution, he had fits of sleepiness. On the day his son died he slept more than ten hours. At the time, his wife had been disturbed by this, but later she realized that it wasn't insensitivity, that there was something deeper at work.

Before dawn the next morning Mesude said she was going to leave the baby with her mother because there was something she had to do in town. She knew several villagers who worked at government offices, companies, shopping centers, and restaurants in the town. These were mostly young men and women who preferred a regular salary to the hardships of fishing, and had taken jobs as security guards, clerks, or cashiers. That day Mesude was going to see Kübra, who worked as a janitor at the public hospital. They'd made arrangements the previous day. Mesude sat on the right side of the bus, leaned her head against the window, and stared vacantly at the sea until they reached the town. Her head banged against the window every time the bus hit a pothole or a bump. The sun was directly above her as she walked to the hospital. It was one of the hottest days of the summer, and it seemed as if it was going to get hotter still. The asphalt was almost at the point of melting.

As always, the hospital was very crowded. People waiting in long lines in the corridors, exhausted doctors and nurses rushing here and there, desperate people, some of them in tears, seeking help...Mesude suddenly felt overwhelmed. Her childhood friend Kübra was a small woman with smiling black eyes, one of the village beauties. Because she was a janitor she had access to every part of the hospital. It was clear that everyone liked her. When people saw her in her white apron with her mop and bucket, people asked her how to find this or that department or doctor; some complained they'd been waiting a long time. And the doctors and nurses smiled as they greeted her. When Kübra saw how worried Mesude was, she made an effort to cheer her up.

"If you knew half of what went on here," she said, and proceeded to tell amusing stories. Mesude laughed, but she was too preoccupied with the migrant woman to fully appreciate them. "Did you look into the woman I asked you about? How is she?"

"Of course I asked about her, I even saw her. Thankfully she's no longer in a coma. She's out of intensive care, but she cries all the time, she won't eat, she keeps calling Samir, Samir."

Mesude winced when she heard the name Samir.

Without feeling the need to conceal her concern, Kübra asked, "Mesude, why do you want to see this woman?"

"I just felt like it. My child was lost at sea too."

"I'm sorry, I didn't understand at first. But don't tell anyone."

When they entered a room on the fourth floor. Mesude saw three patients. Two old women and a young woman. The old women looked up apathetically. The dark, young, thin-faced woman peered at them with her large, olive-like eyes. Mesude saw Deniz in the woman's eyes. There was no doubt in her mind that this was the baby's mother. The woman suddenly began speaking in a foreign language, crying and pleading. Even if she didn't understand what the woman was saying, she could see that she was desperate—she could feel the burning pain in her voice. She kept repeating Samir, Samir. One of the other patients said to Kübra, "Could you please move her out of this room, she cries day and night, she even shouts in her sleep, we can't take it anymore, I tell you, we can't take it anymore." The other patient was quite old, nothing but skin and bones, and there was no expression in her hollow eyes.

Kübra said, "Fine, I'll tell the doctors."

Mesude couldn't take her eyes off the Afghan woman. It was as if the pain had seeped into her flesh and bones, had settled into the lines of her face. It wasn't just pain. It was pain mixed with fear and hope—yes, surprisingly, she saw hope. She'd been the same way when she felt the pain of losing Deniz. She still felt that pain; it would never go away. At that moment she perceived the woman as herself. She saw herself lying in that bed and calling out for Deniz. Suddenly she rushed over and hugged the woman. She touched the thin woman's bones. Kübra had trouble pulling her away from the woman, and in the corridor she said, "Are you trying to get me into trouble? I don't want to lose my job because of you."

As she left the hospital, Mesude felt sick. She had trouble overcoming her nausea enough to get on the bus. Sweat dripping from her hair and her brow mixed with her tears.

That night she and her husband had the fiercest argument they'd ever had. When she got home she said, "Mustafa, tomorrow morning we're bringing that baby back. We're going to bring Samir back to his mother."

At first Mustafa was frightened by the decisiveness in her voice and on her face, and then he got angry. "For starters, his name is Deniz. His name is not Samir, do you understand? Listen to me, we're not bringing the baby anywhere, get that through your head."

Mesude looked him straight in the eye and said, "No, you listen to me. That baby has a mother, I went and saw her today. She's going through the same agony I went through when I lost Deniz. Don't you realize how much the woman is suffering?"

Mustafa grabbed her roughly by the arm. "What!? What did you say? You went to the hospital without telling me? Why did you do that? And without letting me know."

"Don't shout at me, don't you dare raise your voice like that!"

"How could you go see that woman without telling me?" he shouted. His face was strained from anger. He raised his hand as if to hit her.

Mesude raised her voice. "What are you going to do, huh? Are you going to hit me? Go ahead, hit me. I'm not a child thief!"

"Look at this mess," Mustafa shouted, "You can't be a woman and give me a child, and now you're try-ing to give back the son fate gave me as a gift."

Mesude gave him a look of hatred. She felt a wave of heat rising to her head. She wanted to slap his strained face. She almost did it, but she stopped herself at the last moment. She looked him up and down with contempt, went out the door, and slammed it behind her. She was trembling with anger as she made her way to her mother's house. Mustafa had never been this bad before. *We're never going to be able to look each other in the face again, not after this. He almost hit me. Like those men we hear about.*

She wanted to tell her mother about what had happened, she wanted this even though it would upset her, she wanted to vent, but she also wanted her mother to protect her and to help her carry out her decision.

Evening was falling and lights were coming on in the village when she finished telling her mother what had happened. She poured her heart out; she said everything she was thinking about Mustafa. *I'll never look at that man in the face again. It's over.* Her mother, who'd been through so much, listened and tried to calm her. *Hold on, let a couple of days pass, then we'll talk again.* Mesude laughed irritably. Then she laid her head on her mother's lap and stroked Samir Deniz's hair. She knew Mustafa wouldn't have the courage to come to her mother's house that night. And he didn't.

That night she took Deniz in her arms, smelled his neck, caressed him, and sang lullabies all night long. Deniz woke twice. Mesude changed him, gave him his bottle, and then did something that seemed strange even to her. She dripped milk from the bottle onto her nipple and brought the baby's mouth to it. When the baby took the nipple and began sucking greedily on it, she felt an indescribable fullness, a thrill, a delight, but it also brought her fear and pain. She closed her eyes. The feelings spreading from her nipple made her head spin. Deniz was in her arms, a young bride was giving him her breast in that whitewashed house, and soon the man she loved would return from fishing. They would lie on the bed with the baby between them, they would admire him, unable to believe he was theirs. Mustafa looked at her with an expression of gratitude. *You gave me such a wonderful gift... I don't know what to say.* She silenced him by kissing him on the lips. As if any more words would break the spell.

All night she watched the baby sleeping with its arms spread by his side, as if in infinite surrender. She went back and forth between her tenderness for the baby and her anger at Mustafa.

n that windless night Mustafa sat under the vine and drank rakı. He kept filling his glass and emptying it. It went to his head because he was drinking on an empty stomach. He was trying to think of a solution, but he couldn't. For a while he thought about going and banging on his mother-in-law's door. Then when he pictured Mesude's angry face he lost his courage. *I suppose it's over*, he said to himself. He knew that Mesude was patient, but that when she was angry enough she was capable of anything. And this time she was furious.

Toward morning, before dawn, as the sea was getting lighter, the fisherman staggered down the road toward the harbor. He almost fell into the water as he was getting into his boat. This was the first time this had ever happened. That day he went quite far out. Suddenly a light wind woke the sea, and waves began rolling toward the shore. As if the sea were brushing the sleep out of its eyes and stretching. When Mustafa was pulling in his net, he was enraged to see that it was torn in places. The vile puffer fish had damaged his nets again. If the net wasn't thick enough, they could chew their way out of it. He stood, rocking the boat, and shouted, "What kind of creature are you, puffer fish, God damn you, I hope you pop like a balloon!"

These monsters were swarming in from unknown seas like a plague sent by God, threatening their livelihood. They had jaws like a clamp and sharp teeth. They could cut fishing lines, damage nets, swallow any fish that came near, poison the lives of the fishermen. Mustafa still hadn't bought thick nets, and they were snapping off the reel lines. He was going to buy thick nets, of course, but with all the confusion of the past days he hadn't had the chance. Thankfully, he'd brought the steel lines the Stutterer had given him. Those jaws could chew through a can, so nothing except steel would work. Indeed, some of the bigger puffer fish could break the steel lines as well.

Once Mustafa had picked up a puffer fish to examine it. The moment he touched it, it puffed out like a balloon. It frightened him to see how its face became so crocodilian. Then it almost took off his finger. When Mustafa caught a puffer fish, he would beat it to death. He would beat five or ten of them at a time—he took tremendous pleasure in watching their puffed-up bodies explode, exuding some kind of bile as their internal organs spilled out. The deck would be covered in blood. Blood would splatter all over him. He would bellow as he battered them to pieces. A delight in violence that he'd never known before would rise within him like dark water. He got caught in a spiral in which violence begot more violence.

The massacre continued for some time. Then he heard a voice calling to him from nearby.

"Mustafa. Mustafa! Hey, what's going on?" He made an effort to pull himself together, and when he looked up he recognized his friend Çiroz. He was knee-deep in crushed fish, and his face was covered in blood. "What's going on, Mustafa? Everyone is wondering about you. We saw you from our boats and couldn't believe the state you're in."

"What's it to you?" shouted Mustafa. "What business is it of yours? Go away and leave me alone."

"Mustafa, brother, you're losing it, look, the other guys are coming too." Mustafa heard the sound of the motors; they were approaching quickly. Çiroz said, "We're not going to leave you alone. Be a man, listen, come over to my boat, you're not going to be able to resist all of us."

Mustafa was suddenly overcome by exhaustion. His arms hung limply by his side. He looked as if he was about to collapse on the deck. Çiroz pulled up, put one foot on Mustafa's boat, grabbed him by the arm, pulled him onto his boat, and sat him down. Then he started the motor and sped away. The other fishermen would bring Mustafa's boat back to the harbor. He signaled to them. Mustafa sat in the stern, staring down at his feet. Yusuf handed him a jerrican of water and said, "Wash your face, man, don't let anyone else see you like that. And isn't that fish poisonous?"

Mustafa did as he was told. He took the jerrican and washed his face a bit, and then he froze. He sat perfectly still, without making a sound. When they reached the village, Çiroz dragged Mustafa home as everyone looked on. He wanted to get Mustafa to eat something. Before he had a chance to do this, Mustafa flung himself onto the bed and fell into a deep sleep. Çiroz covered him and then left. He didn't look for Mesude, because the whole village knew they'd separated and that Mesude was staying with her mother.

The following day Mesude took the baby to the hospital, her heart beating like a bird caught in a trap. She climbed to the fourth floor, kissed Samir Deniz one last time before entering the woman's room, and then went and placed the baby in the woman's arms before she even understood what was happening. The woman's eyes grew wide in disbelief as she looked at the baby. The woman looked into her eyes—she seemed to want to ask something. Then, as she extended her hand, her dark, bony arm emerged from her hospital gown. Mesude felt she was both asking for help and expressing gratitude. She trembled in terror, torn between regret and happiness, and without another word she left the room as if she were fleeing. In the corridor she could hear the woman shouting Samir's name. She rushed down the stairs, then walked and walked in the hot sun without any idea of where she was going. As if her brain was numbed. She sat on a garden wall in a neighborhood she didn't know. She sat there for hours. Then finally it occurred to her to take the bus and return to her mother's house.

*I*n the morning the police came to get Mustafa from his house and Mesude from her mother's house. The two of them sat across from each other in the van. They each had a policeman sitting next to them. Their eyes didn't meet; both of them stared at the floor. They didn't see the villagers who'd gathered to whisper and stare on both sides of the road.

Mesude told the prosecutor everything in minute detail. She didn't put the blame on Mustafa alone, she took responsibility for her part in everything.

Mustafa felt as if he were tumbling down a bottomless well, and he cringed as the prosecutor rebuked him harshly for having lied.

In the end the prosecutor sent them to court, with a request that they be charged with kidnapping, illegal detention, perjury, and several other charges. After a brief hearing, Mesude was released pending trial and Mustafa was sent to jail.

ustafa had a strange feeling as he entered the jail, as if all of this was happening to someone else and he was observing it from outside. The guard looked at the thin-faced prisoner with sunken cheeks and asked, "What happened?" "I don't know," he answered. "What do you mean you don't know? What did you do to end up in here?" He shrugged and said, "Nothing." The guard mumbled something, then unlocked the barred door and pushed him in. It was clear to him that this weather-beaten man was a fisherman: he looked as if he was constantly scanning the horizon. These seamen were always a bit strange. The guard had learned this over the years.

The four men in the small cell looked up when he entered. One of them said, "Welcome. God help you, brother."

He sat on the bunk they pointed to. The other prisoners had brewed tea, and they offered him some. They seemed like harmless men. All of them except one were about the same age as him. The one who was a bit older had a face like a fox and didn't inspire trust. In fact, he exuded deceit. His eyes were close together and were constantly darting about. He didn't look like someone who'd ended up there through bad luck; he seemed as if this was something he was used to. Of course he asked the first question a newcomer is asked.

"So, how did you end up here?"

"I don't know. I'm just a fisherman."

"Yes, but fishing isn't against the law."

"Of course not. I found dead bodies in the sea. The bodies of migrants, their inflatable boat capsized in a storm."

"Oh no, were they the ones who fell off our boat, I wonder?"

"Were you the one who was smuggling those poor people?"

"Yes, that's what I do, but sometimes we have bad luck."

Of the other cellmates, one was in because of a traffic accident, one for breach of contract, and the other for threatening his landlord. None of them were professional criminals. But the older man clearly was. He was quite open about it; he didn't try to conceal it. He said he'd been in prison several times. Mustafa pictured the bodies in the sea. He felt as if he should be angry at the man, but in fact he felt apathetic.

"The real problem is with the people in charge," the man was saying. There was a strange tone of grievance in his voice. "Sometimes they allow us to take the migrants across, they give us permission, and then they suddenly forbid us. It's all about politics. We're the ones who suffer."

"And the migrants," said one of the others.

"Of course," said the man, "it's rough for them, but what can we do? We bring inflatable boats from Istanbul. They go for seven or eight thousand dollars, and of course we have other expenses too—we based our plans on the fact that the government was allowing it, even encouraging it. Then suddenly they shut us down." He was speaking like a businessman talking about an economic crisis. "But we'd already brought so many people to the coast, we'd already spent a lot of money, so we just loaded people into the boats and set off. Most of the time we evade the Greek coast guard and land them safely in isolated coves on one or another of the islands. From time to time a storm blows up—you never know what the sea is going to be like."

"Why do these boats sink so often?" asked Mustafa. "I suppose you load too many people into them."

The man bowed his head. "Yes, I won't lie, we try to take as many people as we can. We load the boats beyond capacity, otherwise we end up losing money." He looked at Mustafa, then tried to continue in a more convincing manner. "Not every trip is successful. Sometimes the Greek patrol boats chase us back into Turkish waters."

"What happened this last time?" asked Mustafa.

The man sighed. "It was a disaster. Pakistanis, Afghans, Syrians...There were too many people. We were just about to reach shore when we were caught by a Greek patrol. They wouldn't let us land; they towed us back toward Turkish waters. We didn't know what to do or where to go, so we decided to try to reach another island. Night had fallen, and the wind was getting stronger. We couldn't find a place to land on the other islands either. Meanwhile the children on the boat were starting to get restless. There was a baby crying, and then the women started shouting. They started to panic. This made things even more dangerous: we tried to get them to calm down and sit in their places. Then the wind got even stronger, and we capsized."

"Weren't there any life jackets?"

"There were. Some people survived, some even made it to Greece, but the rest disappeared into the sea. Most of them had life jackets...Fate. It was their time."

Mustafa wanted to be angry at the man, to be very angry, but he was overcome with apathy and lethargy.

"And the baby," he managed to say.

"What baby?"

"It seems a baby was rescued."

"Thank God." A smile spread across the man's face. "So the baby was rescued. It's a miracle. A young woman boarded with a baby. From time to time she covered herself with a blanket so she could feed the baby. She had a small inflatable boat with her. A child's toy boat. When it was clear we were going to sink, she tied the baby into this boat. She jumped into the water. The last I saw her, she was trying to push that little boat. Then she disappeared into the darkness."

They listened to him in dismay, then asked how these thousands of migrants had come there.

Then the man told them about a world they knew nothing about. "The people who come from Africa are always brought to Iran first. The people fleeing war in Afghanistan and Pakistan also go to Iran. The smugglers here coordinate with the smugglers in Iran. They walk groups of migrants for days through the mountains until they reach the border. Sometimes they get caught by the authorities. People run off in all directions and get lost in the mountains. They're either eaten by wolves or freeze to death. Those who make it across are delivered to the Turkish smugglers, and then they're brought to a safe house. If they're lucky they're given hot food. It's never clear how long they have to stay. Then they bring them to us here on the coast. This is a large, international operation. There's a lot of money involved."

That night Mustafa lay on his bunk and sank into a deep, dreamless sleep. In the morning he wasn't woken by his cellmates talking, or the music on the radio or the guard's voice or the noise outside. He didn't even think of Mesude. Then an interesting thing happened. Just before he was woken he had a brief dream. In the dream a snake was biting his leg. It happened just the way it had when he was a child.

Three friends had gone to the deserted island across from İncilipinar. They climbed toward a monastery that had been abandoned for centuries. The island was covered with scrub. There were no paths, and they had to make their way through the bushes and shrubs. Just as they were nearing the top, Mustafa saw a spotted green snake climbing his leg. He shouted and started hitting it with his stick. As the snake fled into the bushes, he felt a burning sensation. He'd been bitten near his ankle. His two friends brought him down to the shore and laid him in their little boat. Yılmaz immediately tied a cloth tightly around the bite. Then they began rowing across. Fortunately it was close, and they started shouting to the people on the shore that their friend had gotten a snakebite.

Mustafa's face had turned red, and he was sweating. It hadn't taken them more than five minutes to row across, but in that time his fever had risen and he was beginning to faint.

Suddenly, time has passed. This incident is in the past. The three friends are reminiscing about it, saying it was a good thing they shouted to people on the shore. It was a good thing that Zübeyde the midwife heard them and come running with her herbs. She sucked out the poison, cleaned the wound, applied balm, and bandaged it. All the older villagers knew about medicinal herbs. Yılmaz kept shaking him by the shoulder: "Wake up, it's dangerous to sleep when you've been bitten by a snake."

Just then Mustafa opened his eyes and looked to see who was trying to wake him. Then he realized he was in prison, and that one of his cellmates was trying to wake him. "Your lawyer is here, he wants to see you, come on, get up."

Mustafa pulled himself together and splashed water on his face. Then the guard took him to the visiting area. This was the lawyer he'd met when the prosecutor sent him to court. He was a young man. He said his name, but it didn't register in his befuddled mind. He seemed like a well-intentioned man. Mustafa asked if he would have to pay him any money. He had no money to pay the lawyer—he hadn't been out fishing for some time.

"No," said the lawyer with an understanding smile, "As I told you before, you won't have to pay me anything. I've been appointed by the bar association to defend you."

Mustafa was relieved.

The lawyer said, "Your position isn't as bad as you might think. Your intentions were good, you saved a child's life, and you didn't try to flee or alter evidence. You're a fisherman who's respected in his community. I think the prosecutor could have dismissed the charges, but..." The lawyer paused and smiled slightly. Mustafa looked at him as if he wanted to ask a question. The lawyer spoke as if he were telling a friend a secret: "I think he was angry about your previous statements. We have seven days to appeal. And we will appeal. I think we can rely on article 30/4 of the penal code."

"What is that? I hope it doesn't mean I have to pay a fine."

The lawyer paused and smiled, then said, "Your actions constitute an unavoidable mistake rather than deliberate intent to break the law. Don't worry."

Mustafa didn't understand how saving a baby could be considered a mistake.

"I'll cite this article and request that charges against you and your wife be dropped."

Mustafa's head was spinning. He didn't want to think about anything. He returned to his cell, briefly explained the situation to his cellmates, ate the sandwich and drank the tea they gave him, thanked them, and lay back down on his bunk. As if he were fleeing the thoughts that were swirling through his head. It was dangerous to think and to remember, he felt this, and he was trying to escape. Or else the dark void within would swallow him.

He feared this void, but also seemed to want to fall into it. Whatever was going to happen, he wanted it to happen and be done with. He felt like a fish struggling for air in the hold of his boat, writhing and flicking its tail. The water that drowned people kept the fish alive, and the air that kept people alive drowned the fish. This was unfathomable. The child who had brought happiness to others had brought them disaster. Deniz had spent months in the fluids in his mother's belly; why hadn't he drowned then? Why did he drown in the sea later? Suddenly he realized he was thinking again, and in panic he tried to chase the thoughts away.

Mustafa's friends realized that he was in an even worse state than he'd been in before. They didn't know if it was because they'd taken the baby or because he and Mesude had separated. After he got out of jail they tried to include him, to get him to eat and drink with them on the beach, but to no avail. The court dismissed the charges against him, just as the young lawyer had said they would. But in spite of this Mustafa was like a ghost. It was as if his soul had departed. He would set out in his boat before dawn, return in the afternoon to sell his fish, and then go home. It goes without saying that he didn't speak to anyone.

Some of the elders of the village took Mesude and Mustafa aside. They talked to them and tried to find a way to get them back together, but again to no avail. Neither of them had any intention of making peace. Especially not Mesude.

In time the village became accustomed to the situation. They tended to see everything that happened as normal. The village was like the sponges that divers brought up from the depths. It absorbed and digested pain, sorrow, delight, and disaster. Even the strangest incident was met with the phrase "of course." Of course he murdered his wife; he died when the roof collapsed on him, of course; the boy eloped with the girl, of course. Nothing was astounding, everything was normal.

Mustafa didn't find any more dead bodies in the sea, but a dead dolphin did get caught in some other fishermen's nets. They cut their nets and brought it to the surface in the hope that it would live, but it didn't—the beautiful creature just sank into the depths. Mustafa watched after it, thinking about the strange things called life and death and passion. His anger at the puffer fish had lessened, his anger about everything had lessened. The seagull that had taken to landing on his boat seemed to understand this. It would perch on the prow, looking around with its expressionless eyes. When Mustafa tossed it a piece of bread, it would catch it in the air. This became a habit. He'd made a friend.

———

One day he stopped and looked into the dark-blue water gently lapping at the boat. He stared into it for a long time, as if he could see the bottom. Then he slowly lowered himself into the water, holding on to the side of the boat. He went in as far as his chin and hung there from the boat for quite some time. He imagined letting go and sinking into the sweet coolness of the sea. It would have been an easy death. A fitting end to a pointless life. He felt no fear: letting go would mean liberation. Yet it seemed as if a voice in his head was telling him not to. He asked the voice why he shouldn't, what possible reason he shouldn't. But the voice continued stubbornly buzzing in his head. It might have been saying *It's a sin.*

He didn't know how long he stayed in the water, perhaps an hour, perhaps longer. When he heard a motor approaching, he realized it was too late even to die. He hadn't even managed to die like a man. His friends had been keeping an eye on him—they must have worried when they didn't see him in the boat. He had no choice but to pull himself back into his boat. Then he lay down on the deck in his wet clothes. Could someone who knew how to swim succeed at drowning himself? Even if he made the decision, would his body obey? If it were possible, then he could kill himself by lying in bed and holding his breath. He was thinking about pointless things. He'd stayed in the water so long for nothing. Whatever he did, his body was going to hang on to life.

It was only when he looked around that he saw how far he'd drifted. The current had carried the boat a considerable distance. "Hey," shouted Yusuf, "are you going to seek asylum in Greece? If you go any farther you'll have a patrol boat on top of you." He didn't answer; he just started the motor and steered the boat back to the village.

The thing that caused Mustafa the most pain at home was the slightly bitter, intoxicating smell of the jasmine that Mesude had planted with her delicate fingers. Mesude had a green thumb; everything she planted thrived. She'd trained the jasmine to climb the walls of the house. It had given him so much pleasure to watch those little white flowers bloom—he admired the loving attention his wife gave to her plants. One day, when Mesude saw him running his hand over the jasmine, she'd said, "The feel of the flowers is even more beautiful than their appearance."

Now the smell of that jasmine was like a stone falling into the still water of the well within him. It was as if Mesude had left behind her twin. She'd slipped away from him like a fish that had snapped the line, and he would never find her again. One night, after tossing and turning for some time, he'd rushed out into the garden to pull the jasmine down. He couldn't do it, of course; as soon as he touched the vine, damp with dew, he felt as if he were touching Mesude's skin. Those flowers were the last link he had to Mesude. He even missed her hands. As for the baby, he tried not to think about him at all. Whenever he started to wonder where the baby was and who was looking after him, he would fall into a deep sleep and escape into the mysterious darkness. The days, the weeks, and even the months ran into each other.

The people who had lived in these villages for generations had never thought about who owned the sea, the mountains, and the forests. The little houses and the gardens had owners, but everything else belonged to God. How could nature, the air, and the water have owners? But it seemed they did. Suddenly the villages found themselves under assault from land, from sea, and from the air. The world they were accustomed to was different; the sea couldn't belong to anyone; the sky, the forest, the mountains, and waterfalls and springs were things that could not be owned. They were all God-given blessings. Then suddenly strangers had come from far away to assault the earth and the water.

Somehow they simply couldn't fathom this. The fish farms had taken ownership of the sea. They'd established fish prisons in which millions of fish darkened the waters, leaving a foul smell hanging over the bays. Mustafa didn't go into the bays anymore, and neither did his friends. Bays that had been as clear as glass when he was a child had become lakes of gray sludge overhung with a heavy, nauseating smell. They poured all kinds of chemicals into the water, and tons of chemicals sank to the bottom, killing the sea.

By law these fish farms were supposed to be on the open sea, but who paid attention to that? Those who were able to pay could put their farms wherever they wanted. They were all outsiders. They weren't from the Aegean. They'd spoken to the reporters who came to the village. They constantly sent petitions to the municipality, but even if the newspapers printed the story, no one seemed to care. These articles and petitions had changed nothing. The villagers could do nothing but watch their sea die a slow death. On top of that, strange fish had come from afar. These foreign people and foreign fish resembled each other. They were all rapacious and destructive.

Some mining companies had set their sights on the pine-covered mountains. They'd cut swaths of trees to build roads, and they'd begun digging holes in search of minerals. There was even one company that was going to use cyanide to extract gold—the villagers had been furious when they heard this. That poison would seep into the groundwater and finish off the villagers and their animals. They held marches to protest this; they submitted complaints and petitions. Once again this produced no results whatsoever. The government had given the companies permission to do whatever they wanted; the mines were protected by armed guards. Every day the women cursed them and their gold for destroying their mountains, streams, and forests. This at least gave them momentary relief.

These weren't the only enemies that had come from afar. They'd heard that a huge hotel was going to be built on the wooded headland to the right of the village. They'd already started cutting trees to build a road. They had graders operating all day. They were going to cut down all the trees. They tried to fool the villagers by telling them that the hotel and the villas would provide work for them.

Once some students came from another city. For days they demonstrated with placards against the cutting of the trees and the use of cyanide. The villagers joined them. The demonstrations were allowed to continue for a couple of days. Then a phalanx of riot police came to disperse the crowd. The students were beaten with truncheons and loaded onto military trucks. The villagers felt sorry for those fresh-faced young men and women.

*O*ne Sunday the leading citizens of the village gathered everyone together under the vines of Gırdinni's coffeehouse. On that bright Sunday morning, men and women arrived dressed in colorful clothes. This old coffeehouse wasn't on the shore: it was inland, on the edge of the village. There was a large open space in front of it. Village weddings were held here too.

As Mesude arrived at the coffeehouse, she remembered their festive wedding. Decorated tables and chairs; the stage, festooned with roses, on which local musicians played; people dancing under the hundreds of lightbulbs that had been strung up; children, all dressed up, running around and whirling with boundless energy; food of all kinds being brought to the tables; glistening rakı glasses; Mesude's white wedding dress, now packed in a chest at home; her heart beating so loudly; how she'd twice repeated "yes" to the registrar; the love and admiration she saw in Mustafa's gray eyes, as well as the surprise and bashfulness...Everyone had a wonderful time. The smells of spring and the crowds of people brought memories of that happy, innocent day when they knew nothing of the pain and misery that was in store for them. Deniz must have been conceived that night, when their bodies melted into each other in the moonlight that streamed through the window, that holy night on which they performed that primitive ritual, both tender and savage, writhing and moaning until morning.

Mesude was brought back to the present when they started passing around newspaper clippings. These were articles about things that had happened in other villages. There were terrible pictures of forests and meadows that had been destroyed. The wholesale destruction of trees, the excavation of hellish pits, quarries carved out of mountainsides. The mines had made the countryside look like a battlefield. These pictures brought tears to their eyes. If that wasn't enough, they'd built massive, ugly concrete buildings along the shore.

Mustafa thought that these people were more dangerous than the puffer fish, more monstrous, more evil, more destructive. Without letting on, he was watching Mesude in the distance. He could see her reading one of the cuttings. In other circumstances she would prattle on to Mustafa about what she thought, but now she was leaning over to tell her mother something. Suddenly he felt like walking over, taking Mesude by the hand, and bringing her home. He didn't of course, he just sat there hoping to catch a glance from her.

At one point Captain Tahsin took the microphone and addressed the villagers: "You've seen the situation. If we don't resist, they'll destroy us too, they'll reduce us to ashes." The villagers were horrified by what they'd seen in the newspapers. Then they began discussing what could be done. They were besieged on all sides; they'd even begun to feel the effects of the thermal power plant that had been built a few years ago on the far side of the district. They were under assault from the air as well. Some people were fired up and talking excitedly about putting up resistance, while others talked of what was likely to happen if they resisted.

"The government has given them all permission; they can do what they want. If we resist they'll just send the riot police. We'll be beaten and sent to jail. Isn't that what happens everywhere?"

Çiroz jumped to his feet.

"No!" he shouted. "Some towns and villages were able to get the mining companies to back down. In some places they chained themselves to olive trees to prevent them from being cut down. That is, they went to great lengths, but they did it. We can do that too, no surrender."

Even though they were sitting at the same table, Mustafa didn't take any interest in what he was saying.

He was completely focused on Mesude, who was sitting with her mother. Throughout the meeting she didn't look in his direction—not even a glance out of the corner of her eye. She spent the whole time talking to her mother. When the meeting was over, they got up and left. Mustafa saw Mesude laugh and say something to her mother, and her mother laughed as she answered. On top of this, everyone was aware of the situation. It was clear that they wanted to humiliate him in front of the entire village. It hurt him that his wife had behaved in such a calm, indifferent manner. He was excited. He felt he had to do something, but what? What should he do?

When Çiroz saw Mustafa staring at Mesude and breathing quickly, he signaled to Yusuf and the Stutterer. Mustafa's fists were clenched, and he was still staring. He wasn't aware of his friends or the dispersing crowd.

"We can't just leave it at that," said Yusuf. "We should go somewhere and talk, make a plan."

"Aren't we the young men of the village? Doesn't it fall to us to do something?" said Çiroz.

"Come on, Mustafa!"

Mustafa asked. "What? What are you talking about?"

"What?"

"What do you mean, what?"

"What do you think, come on, get up."

"Where?"

"We were just talking about it all, weren't you paying attention?"

"I was lost in thought, what were you talking about?"

"We're going to go sit down somewhere and make a plan."

"To stand up to the mining companies."

"I can't come," said Mustafa.

His friends voiced their objections.

"Come on, this is something that concerns us all. The future of the village."

"You can't cop out, Mustafa."

They practically forced him to get up from the table. They went to a hidden cove behind the wooded headland where they were going to build the hotel. On the way, Çiroz bought rakı and some snacks. They sat and talked until evening. Their enemy was like an octopus. It had many arms: Where were they to start? At this stage it didn't seem as if taking on the mining companies made sense—they had armed guards. And it would be some time before mining operations began.

"Then," said Çiroz, "it makes sense to begin with our livelihood, with the sea."

"But what can we do?" asked Yusuf.

The Stutterer struggled to say something, but Yusuf lost patience and blurted, "We start with the fish farms, of course." The Stutterer gave his friend an offended look. He never allowed him to finish a sentence.

They decided they would sabotage the fish farms. They'd start with the largest ones. They would destroy them one by one and reclaim their sea. God would help them because they were in the right. They egged each other on. The rakı made it seem as if everything would be easy. A sense of bravery rose within them. It was Mustafa, who had *lost his wits*, they said behind his back, who brought them to their senses.

"Do you think it will be that easy? They have guards, there are cameras, they send divers down to check. They've sunk millions into those farms. How are we going to do this?"

The three of them raised their glasses in unison. "We trust you, Mustafa. You're the best diver in these parts. You know every rock and every hollow. We'll help you, and you'll dive. We'll start with the easiest one."

This confidence was the only positive thing in Mustafa's disordered life. Especially after Mesude had been so disdainful to him, the idea of being the savior of the village began to appeal to him. The emptiness he'd felt since Mesude left him, the sense of being nothing more than a breathing, walking shell, was becoming unbearable. The night before, he'd dreamt about a wedding. At the same place they'd had their wedding, under the bare lightbulbs. Mesude was wearing a veil, she was getting married, but the face of the man next to her wasn't visible, that is, it wasn't him. He approached and saw that the man had a shark's mouth. He had human eyes but a shark's mouth. He woke in terror to find that his pillow was wet. He got up and drank a large glass of cold water. The walls were closing in on him; he could no longer fit in the house.

He went down to the harbor. He untied his boat, which was wet with dew, and began rowing. He remembered a song called "In the Middle of the Sea." He wondered where "the middle of the sea" was. Perhaps it was here. He murmured the song as he dropped anchor. Then he lay down in the damp boat. He looked at the stars until he drifted off to sleep. Sometime later he was woken by a kind of scratching sound, and then he felt a sharp pain in his ear. He jumped up. At first he didn't know what had happened, but when he grabbed his flashlight he saw one of the brown crabs he'd caught the day before and tossed into the boat. They were delicious, and the restaurants paid good money for them. He picked up the crab that had bitten his ear and looked at it. *You're right, brother. If I were a crab, I would have done the same thing. Maybe I separated you from your wife. Go on, go in peace.*

He threw the crab back into the sea.

As he was mooring the boat, he saw Ömer approaching. This time he had no stamp, and he wasn't blowing a whistle. Mustafa suddenly felt he wasn't going to be able to deal with Ömer. He was in such a bad mood he didn't feel he could stand this boy he was usually happy to see. He wasn't in the mood for the boy's games. The boy came very close to him, looking up at him with a serious expression. There was something strange about him; he was staring with his fishlike eyes.

"What's up?" asked Mustafa anxiously. "Did something happen?"

"You're a donkey."

Mustafa was surprised. "OK, so I'm a donkey. I'm busy now; we can talk later."

"Yes, you're a donkey, you're even more of a donkey than the donkey in our stable. And…and you're stupid."

Why was the boy so angry?

"Yes, I'm a donkey," Mustafa said calmly. "But this donkey needs to go home now. Can we talk tomorrow?"

"No!"

"Why not, Ömer? Do you have a problem?"

"Yes, I do."

"What is it, go ahead, tell me."

Mustafa saw that the boy was on the verge of tears. It must have been something serious. He felt bad and put his hand on the boy's shoulder.

"Don't touch me. Aren't you ashamed of leaving Mesude?"

Mustafa was astounded. The boy continued. "You're a donkey for leaving Mesude! Do you understand, you're a donkey."

He knew Ömer was very fond of Mesude. Whenever he came to the house, she would give him the cola and chips she bought specially for him. Ömer would look at her in gratitude and smile. Once he'd impulsively kissed her on the cheek. *The boy's an angel*, Mesude used to say, *a real angel*. The whole village loved the boy, but Mesude's affection was different.

Ömer stared at him with a deep frown. Mustafa took him seriously for the first time.

"I didn't leave her, Ömer. She's the one who decided to go. She left me."

"Who knows what you did to her."

"I didn't do anything."

"You did, you must have done something to Mesude."

"Why would I do anything to her?"

"Because you're a donkey!" shouted the boy, and then he ran off. He seemed to be crying.

As Mustafa made his way home, he thought, The boy's right, I'm a donkey. He must have heard people talking about the separation. He's the only one in the village who said anything to my face. The boy's right.

esude's grandmother's fairy tales were famous throughout the village, and indeed even in neighboring villages. On winter evenings when the men went to the coffeehouse, the women and children would gather around the olive wood fire, sip sage tea, and listen to stories about giants, princesses, people transformed into animals, animals transformed into humans, sultans whose touch turned everything into gold, and treacherous viziers. They couldn't get enough of the story of how, on a night when the full moon was shining like mother of pearl, the Prophet raised his index finger and split the moon in two. The old women would shout, *God is great*, and begin crying. They couldn't quite explain to the younger women why they cried. Perhaps it was the melancholy of being closer to death, perhaps a feeling of terror, of fear.

Some of her grandmother's stories were about Hārūn ar-Rashīd, and some were from Solomon. Mesude's favorite was the story of the child who was abandoned by his mother the queen and raised by a servant.

A kingdom faces rebellion. The queen flees with her husband, leaving behind her baby. The baby's caretaker can't bear to leave him behind, so she takes him and raises him on her own. Years later the queen returns and wants her child back. The caretaker refuses. After all, she's the one who rescued the baby and struggled to raise him, and she regards him as her own child.

When they go before King Solomon, he says, "Draw a circle on the floor. His mother will pull one arm and his stepmother will pull the other arm. I'll give the child to whoever manages to pull him out of the circle."

They do as Solomon tells them. They each seize an arm and begin pulling. But when the stepmother sees that this is hurting the child, she lets go. She can't bear to hurt him. She says she would rather the queen have him than see him torn apart. The queen is happy that she pulled the child out of the circle, but Solomon says, "The child belongs to the stepmother. She was more protective of him than his real mother. She was afraid he would be hurt. Because she raised him, kept him alive. She is now his real mother."

In fact it had no resemblance to her own real story—the poor migrant woman didn't leave the baby behind and flee—but she identified with the step-mother in the story. She and Mustafa had rescued the baby and made the effort to bring him back to life.

The moment she thought of Mustafa, she said, "Damn him." She couldn't get over her anger. Not only had he insulted her womanhood, he'd raised his hand to her. How could she forget that? She couldn't remember a moment when her honor had been more wounded. *He went crazy*, she told her mother, *I think Mustafa definitely lost his mind. He would never do anything like that to me, but the baby unbalanced him. Anyway, he can go to hell*. Mesude wanted a divorce. Her mother did her best to get her to change her mind, but then she gave up and began to support the idea of divorce. *There's another fate for the most beautiful divorcée in the village*, she said, but Mesude had nothing like that in mind. *You didn't marry again and neither will I*. She always stood behind her decisions. She was much stronger than Mustafa.

It wasn't that she didn't still have feelings, but she wouldn't allow her heart to soften. She was resolute.

———

*O*ne afternoon she was hanging laundry in the garden. Ever since childhood, the smell of laundry that had dried in the sun made her happy. As she was hanging the laundry, an official black car pulled up in front of the garden gate. A man and a woman, both of them civil servants, entered the garden, asked her name and surname, checked her identity card, and said they would like to have a word with her. Mesude was alarmed. At first she thought it was something to do with the court or the prosecutor, or with Mustafa. Had he filed for divorce? This was the first time she'd had government officials at her house. Or had something happened to Mustafa? Were they bringing her bad news? Suddenly she felt terrified. Mustafa, she thought, my Mustafa, oh my Mustafa.

*T*he officials said they were from the Muğla Migration Administration Unit. Mesude and her mother welcomed them in. As he was entering, the young man patted the basil plant and smiled, the rich smell of basil wafting through the air.

While her mother went in to make coffee, the officials explained the situation to Mesude.

The illegal migrants—they used the term "irregular migrants"—Zilha Sherif and her child Samir were being held in a Migration Administration shelter in Ula. Mesude realized they weren't bringing her bad news about Mustafa. At first she felt relieved, but then her heart began to beat even faster. The officials began telling her that three days ago the migrant woman had approached them through a lawyer with a request. Mesude was beside herself with excitement. Her heart was beating so loudly it was drowning out the man's voice; she couldn't hear him properly. At the same time she kept turning to look toward the kitchen. She didn't want her mother to hear what they were telling her. She didn't want anyone to know. She didn't want anyone to hear about it. At least not for a while. She wanted to think and fully grasp what they'd said before she talked to anyone about it.

When Raziye Hanım came in with the coffee, they'd finished telling her what they'd come to say, and they'd begun conversing about the village. Mesude could barely hear them. *What's happening*, she kept asking herself, *what's happening?* Bright sunlight reflected from the window was blinding her, clouding her mind, and the smell of basil had become stronger. Are we a family, she wondered, are we a family? Then when she saw her mother and the guests looking at her strangely, she realized she'd spoken these words aloud. "I'm sorry, I don't know why I said that, I'm...surprised and confused." Then she rubbed her eyes with her fists to keep the tears from flowing out.

After the guests left, she had to spend quite some time dealing with her mother. The poor woman was trying to understand what was going on, but her daughter wasn't giving her any explanation. "It's nothing, they just came to give me some information," was all she said. As Mesude tried to fend off her mother's questions, she kept asking herself the same question: *Are we a family, are we a family?* She felt on the verge of fainting.

She also felt as if she were imagining the whole scene. She could hear her mother's voice saying "Mesude, what happened, you're scaring me." Then she felt a coolness on her temples and wrists, and the smell of cologne wafted to her. Her mother was rubbing her wrists. *Pull yourself together, you say they didn't tell you anything important, so why are you in such a state?* While Raziye was making coffee, she'd heard the names Zilha and Samir but hadn't been able to understand anything else. And the officials hadn't seemed as if they were bringing bad news. Or were they so accustomed to giving people bad news that they'd developed an indifferent attitude?

"Mother," Mesude heard herself saying, "I'm not feeling well..." She couldn't move. Her mother hurriedly opened windows to let in fresh air. She heard the tap running in the kitchen, and then her mother put a glass to her lips. She took sips of the cool well water. The smells of basil and cologne battled with each other. Both smells nauseated her, and so did the sun. As she stretched herself out on the sofa, the distress, sorrow, pain, and fear of the past months seemed to form into a ball that was stuck in her throat. A series of brief images kept flashing through her mind: Mustafa, the police, the neighbors, Mustafa, the hospital, the prosecutor, Mustafa again, the jail, the fight, Mustafa's raised hand. The willpower that had kept her on her feet and her emotions at bay seemed to crumble, and she was aware that tears were pouring from her eyes.

At about three in the morning the sea was calm and the village was asleep. Four young fishermen silently rowed Çiroz's boat away from the shore. In order to avoid drawing suspicion to themselves and to the village, they'd decided not to sabotage the huge fish farm near the village but a smaller farm further away. Their sharp knives and saws were ready. As they moved through the water on that moonless night, they felt as if they were embarking on a great adventure. Even Mustafa felt as if there was a new excitement in his life. He'd done a few dives and seen the state the poor fish were in. The fry were poured into the pools from tanks. They were only a millimeter long, and a million of them weighed less than a kilo. The farm owners filled the cages with sea bass and sea bream fry. When the fish grew there was no room for them to move: the ones on the bottom were crushed, and the fish were sickened by parasites and microbes. He'd even seen blind fish. They stretched nets over these cages. Birds who dove to catch fish got caught in these nets, and their necks would break as they struggled to free themselves. As Mustafa thought about this, he remembered the puffer fish he'd crushed. But those fish were monsters. They needed to be destroyed. Nevertheless, he was still ashamed of what he'd done. He'd been out of his mind.

Mustafa was silent the whole way. Indeed, no one spoke, or even smoked a cigarette. He just stared into the dark water and thought dark thoughts. Did the attitude Mesude took toward him that day mean that they'd reached the point of no return? How could that possibly be? What had happened to them for things to end up like this? He wished he'd gone and sat with her. What could she have done? When everyone was leaving I could have taken her by the hand and brought her home, he thought. She wouldn't have refused to come. Or would she have? What would have happened if she'd freed her hand and gone with her mother? And in front of the entire village? For a moment he supposed it might be because of her mother, that she was brainwashing her daughter. Was that why she'd treated him like a stranger?

He knew he'd behaved badly—he'd long since regretted what he'd done. But confessing this was difficult for him. Husbands and wives have fights sometimes. There was no need to blow things out of proportion.

Then he felt guilty when he remembered that he'd said harsh things about her womanhood and her personality and that he'd raised his hand to her. He wouldn't have hit her, of course he wouldn't have; he would never hurt her, it was just that he was so angry. In fact he'd restrained himself to a degree he would never have for anyone else. If it had been anyone but Mesude, he wouldn't have held himself back.

Thinking about these things and making excuses for himself didn't change anything. He'd lost his wife because he wanted a child, and he felt a searing regret. He reached down and put his hand in the sea. The dark water was lukewarm. He thought the sea would remain warm until November. Then he remembered how his son had trailed his hand in the water that day. "Look, Father, look. Look at how beautiful it is." He pulled his hand out of the water as if he'd touched fire.

These fish farms had sleeping quarters and armed guards. About half an hour later, when they reached the fish farm, the lights in the sleeping quarters were out. It was clear that the watchmen were sleeping. In any event, the worst that ever happened was minor theft. They approached the nets silently in the dark. Mustafa slid into the water without a sound, almost without leaving even a ripple. Despite the pitch darkness he didn't light a lamp. He was going to feel around for the net. As he dove, he sensed that there were huge schools of fish around him. Fish were touching his hands and arms and legs. As if he were a large fish. Schools of mullet and sardines would swim to the cages. They were attracted by the feed. Once he'd gone deep enough, he swam toward the net; soon his hand touched it. He pulled out the large, sharp knife he'd strapped to his leg. He began cutting the net with it. They'd chosen a sea bass farm. The sea bream farms had thicker nets because the fish tried to chew their way out. He struggled to cut a few large openings. He felt that there were fish surging out of these openings. There were now more fish around him. Then the fish began pouring out. He had probably cut enough openings, but he swam to the left to cut more. From time to time he rose silently to the surface to fill his lungs. He finally decided he'd cut enough holes. There was now a storm of fish around him, and they were dragging him. He didn't know where they were dragging him, under the sea. It was no longer possible for him to approach the net. He couldn't swim against such a powerful storm.

He rose to the surface. He'd stayed under a long time and was beginning to get dizzy. He tried to breathe silently in the darkness, but he had to take a large gasp and fill his lungs. Little by little he calmed down, and his breathing became regular. He looked around for the boat, but he couldn't see it in the darkness. After a while, though, it began to seem as if finding the boat would be impossible. He didn't know which side of the cage it was on, or how close it was. He cooed softly like a dove, hoping he wouldn't wake the guards. A little later he felt a tremendous relief when he heard the swish of oars and Çiroz whispering. *Mustafa, Mustafa.* They pulled him into the boat and rowed away before anyone heard them. They'd brought down one of the fish farms.

The hot linden tea her mother made for her calmed Mesude's nerves enough for her to drift into a deep sleep. Her dreamless sleep was so deep that she wasn't even aware of her mother coming in and out of the room. In the morning she woke to the light coming in through the window and the sounds of the sparrows and pigeons. She'd recovered from her crisis of the previous day, but she felt a bit tired. And she still felt as if she were in a dream. Or was it a nightmare?

She and her mother had breakfast in silence. Later, when they were drinking coffee on the porch in the shade of the pink bougainvillea, she said, "Mother, we have to talk. We have to decide what to do."

———

Yes, I hope so, I have no idea what's going on." Mesude gave her mother an understanding smile. She felt better, as if she'd been able to pull her thoughts together. She decided to delay the conversation a little.

Mesude always weighed everything carefully, working out the variables, and was always confident of her decisions. It wasn't easy for two fish to find each other in the vast sea. She'd found Mustafa and married him, and they'd shared good times and bad. Was she going to throw this away because of a moment of anger? Until that terrible, disastrous day he'd never even frowned at her. When they took Deniz for a stroll on the shore in the evening, Mesude used to feel as if the whole village envied them. When they were teaching Deniz to swim, they would play around with him, splashing water on each other to make him laugh, and they changed the lyrics of a popular song to "we got wet in this sea together."

The next morning Mesude said to her mother, "I'm going home, Mother. Mustafa hasn't eaten a proper meal in days. I'm going to cook something, and then I'll give the house a good cleaning."

Her mother wasn't at all surprised. It was as if she'd known what she was going to say. "As you wish, dear."

Mesude left the house and strode through the garden so briskly that the chickens barely managed to get out of her way in time. As autumn approached, the weather was getting softer, the sun was rising in a cloudless sky, and the whitewashed houses of the village were reflected on the surface of the sea. As she walked toward the house she thought, *Mustafa could be anywhere now.* When she got home she was going to call him and say *Bring home a nice fish, boy,* as she used to do in the days when they joked with each other. *Don't you dare be late.* That was all she was going to say. Then she would hang up, as if it were an ordinary day, as if nothing had happened. She was good at reeling in fish, she knew when to let the line out and when to pull it in. She pictured the befuddled expression that appeared on Mustafa's face when there was a situation he didn't quite understand. She couldn't help laughing. She clutched the folder carefully to her chest, as if the baby was in it.

he next morning Mustafa, Çiroz, Yusuf, and the Stutterer huddled together. Someone was looking into the incident at the fish farm, and sooner or later they were going to come to the village. "Whatever happens, don't involve me, don't mention my name, I wasn't there. It's not because of the penalty, there's a much more important reason. This is a matter of life and death, it's that important. Yesterday I didn't care, it didn't matter to me what happened, but some things have changed, I'd be ruined, do you understand me? I'd be ruined."

His friends tried to calm him down. "Fine, Mustafa, what's the matter with you, are you losing your marbles again? We won't say anything."

"I want you to swear," insisted Mustafa, "I want to swear on your children's lives, on the graves of your departed. I want you to put your hand on the Koran."

When Çiroz saw that Mustafa was trembling, that his expression was alternating between gloom and joy, he gestured discreetly for the others to leave him alone. They left.

Çiroz tried to calm him. "Come, sit down and have some tea, you're covered in sweat. You're starting to scare me, Mustafa."

"No, you don't understand, I'm not the person I was, I have a duty, I have a duty. If you were to inform on me…"

"Shut up! Cut it out, are you aware that you're insulting your best friends? Am I a rat, do you think you're the only one who has any honor? Pull yourself together or I'm going to mess you up."

Mustafa shut up. Çiroz was a skinny man, there was no way he could beat Mustafa up, but when he was truly angry he didn't care about anything.

Then Mustafa said, "Fine, I'm sorry, but the situation is really serious. I'm not the person I was, some things have changed."

"What changed? Don't keep repeating the same thing. Man up and tell me what's going on."

"Mesude is back. She's back home, and the baby is coming."

"The baby?" Çiroz sounded surprised. He didn't

understand, but he was curious. "What baby? The migrant baby you brought back from the sea?"

"Of course! Our baby! Our new Deniz. Zilha said that under her present circumstances she couldn't take proper care of the baby. She couldn't provide him with any kind of future."

Çiroz, looking somewhat impatient, asked, "Who's Zilha? Who did she tell this to?"

"She's the mother, the baby's mother. She told the authorities. She said that if they accepted, she wanted to give custody of him to the family who rescued him, who fed him and cared for him and then gave him back to her. That's what she said. The officials came and informed Mesude."

He felt the need to be in motion; he wanted to run. Since the subject had come up, he wanted to tell his friend about his feelings in more detail. He wanted to tell him about how, when he was speaking to Mesude the previous evening, she'd held the folder to her chest so carefully it was as if the baby was in it. He felt he was unable to adequately express his feelings to Çiroz. But still, he could see that his friend was pleased. "In order to be allowed to take custody of him I have to have a clean record," he continued, "I was lucky to be acquitted last time, but if this fish farm business comes out they won't give me the baby. Mesude would never forgive me, and my life would be over. I would be ruined."

Çiroz slapped him on the shoulder, "OK, brother, now tell me the whole story, are we your enemies? I'm really happy about how things turned out. You stay out of trouble now, behave yourself. Are you going out fishing?"

"I can't, I have paperwork to take care of, I have to get a paper from the prosecutor, a bunch of other things. It's not easy."

*T*wo days later Mesude and Mustafa went to Ula, to the old prison, which now served as a Repatriation Center. This was where migrants who were rescued or captured were held until they were sent back to their original countries.

There was smoke in the air from the nearby coal-fired power plant. As they entered the white, two-story building, it struck Mesude that they lived their lives unaware of so much that was going on around them— of the lives, the suffering, of people just next to them. The young lawyer was waiting for them inside. He looked very serious in his suit and carefully knotted tie. Mustafa greeted him with gratitude in his eyes. Even in that important, tense, and exciting moment, when Mesude looked at the handsome lawyer, her feminine intuition told her he would be a good match for Kübra. Would it be possible to introduce them?

An official brought them to a small, well-lit, air-conditioned room. The desk was covered in pink folders, and there was a picture of Atatürk behind it. There was no one at the desk. The lawyer said, *Every migrant who's rescued is brought here.*

"Inside there are security guards, the police guard the outside. The migrants sleep in large rooms. Ten or twenty to a room. They're served three meals a day in the dining hall. They can't leave until they're repatriated."

"Are all of them definitely sent back?" asked Mesude.

"Apart from the Syrians, all of them are sent back. The government allows the Syrians to do business and to work. The other migrants don't get that chance. I wish they did."

"Is that lady going to be sent back?" asked Mustafa.

"Yes, that's the rule."

"What if she can't afford the trip?"

"Then the government pays."

Mustafa and Mesude's eyes met. So it meant the woman was doing this in order not to bring the baby back to Afghanistan. They were both saddened to realize that another person's disaster had brought them happiness.

Then the lawyer told them about some distressing things they would rather not have heard, but that they had to know.

He read from the file, summarizing it from time to time.

A little later they brought in Zilha Sherif. Samir was in her arms. There was a pacifier in his mouth, and he was calm. Zilha was wearing a dark-blue dress with horizontal white stripes. The center must have given it to her. Mesude and Zilha looked each other in the eye. A young man they said was an interpreter came in after her. When they all sat down, a middle-aged woman brought tea in on a tray. For a while nothing was heard but the clinking of spoons and cups. Everyone except the lawyer and the interpreter was staring at their tea. The lawyer wasn't stirring his tea; he didn't take sugar. "We all know why we're here. A native of Afghanistan..."

Just then an official came in. A portly, balding man with a moustache. He was wearing a short-sleeved white shirt and a burgundy tie. When he'd taken a seat, he instructed the lawyer to continue.

The lawyer explained the situation clearly and precisely. Zilha Sherif wanted to leave her son Samir Sherif in foster care with the Sılacı family, should they accept this responsibility. An official application had been made.

The official said, "Yes, the application is being processed. Of course we have to adhere to legal statutes. Even if both sides agree, it's not easy."

Then he turned to Mustafa. "As far as I understand, you want to be this baby's foster parents, is that so?"

Mustafa and Mesude said yes in unison.

"In fact the application was supposed to be made by you rather than by the child's mother, but... We sent you some forms, have you filled them out and had them verified?"

"Yes, prosecutor," said Mustafa.

The man smiled and said, "I'm not a prosecutor." Then he continued, "The law allows you to temporarily take in an irregular migrant child as a foster family in emergency situations."

"Temporarily?" Mustafa sounded anxious.

"For now that's the easiest way; the lawyer will explain. Let's do this first, and then you can apply for permanent custody."

He took the folder Mustafa handed to him, glanced at the forms, and checked the signatures and official stamps. Meanwhile Mesude was looking at Zilha, who didn't look up and didn't take her eyes off the baby in her arms. As she watched the baby looking at the woman and the woman looking at the baby, Mesude felt a strange feeling she couldn't quite describe. The baby was here, next to her. If she reached out she could touch him, but she couldn't touch him, at this moment he was not yet Deniz, he was still Samir. His mother was looking at him and he was looking at his mother. He was looking for her breast: he'd taken out his pacifier, and he seemed slightly irritated. The woman whispered something to the interpreter. The interpreter said the baby was hungry, could she step outside for a moment to feed him?

The woman left, walked down the corridor, and entered a room. Mesude followed her. There were other women in the room; some of them were black and some were white. They all had a look of hopelessness in their eyes. Zilha sat on a bunk and gave the baby her breast. He began sucking eagerly. At that moment Mesude's nipples began to ache. She sat next to the woman. They looked at each other. They had no language in common; they couldn't talk to each other. Mesude put her hand on the woman's thin, bony shoulder, as if to give her strength. The woman turned to her, and they looked into each other's eyes for a time as the baby suckled. Zilha took Mesude's hand and placed it on the baby's head. Mesude was now doing what she'd wanted to do but hadn't been able to. She touched the baby's beautiful head lovingly. She looked at the woman in gratitude. There was deep pain in her eyes, but on her lips there was a faint, doleful, broken smile.

When Mesude looked into her eyes she remembered what the lawyer had said. In Kunduz the Taliban had killed her parents, her husband, and her two brothers. She'd escaped the massacre because she'd brought her newborn baby to the clinic. She felt ashamed. She immediately withdrew her hand from the baby's head. She wanted to flee—she could have gone out the door and ran all the way to the village. She was ashamed, deeply ashamed.

The woman looked at her. They looked into each other's eyes. The women understood each other, felt each other, sensed each other. Zilha took Mesude's hand, squeezed it slightly, nodded, and then once again put her hand on the baby's head. The other women watched this silent ceremony. The smell of coal smoke from outside mixed with the smell of dirty laundry in the room. The two women had talked about everything without uttering a single word. A deep bond had been established between the two mothers, between the entrusting and the entrusted. Promises had been made and sworn to. Mesude tried not to think about what the lawyer had told her, but she didn't succeed. "There's a strong possibility they'll kill her when she returns," he'd said. "That's why the child..."

The midafternoon call to prayer sounded. The mosque must have been close, because the muezzin's voice echoed off the walls. Zilha stood, and they walked back to the office together. The corridor smelled of coal, sour sweat, and whitewash, with a faint whiff of coffee coming from somewhere.

ZÜLFÜ LIVANELI is Turkey's best-selling author and a political activist. Widely considered one of the most important Turkish cultural figures of our time, he is known for his novels that interweave diverse social and historical backgrounds, figures, and incidents, including the critically acclaimed *Bliss* (winner of the Barnes & Noble Discover Great New Writers Award), *Serenade for Nadia* (Other Press, 2020), *Disquiet* (Other Press, 2021), *The Last Island* (Other Press, 2022), *Leyla's House*, and *My Brother's Story*, which have been translated into thirty-seven languages, won numerous international literary prizes, and been turned into movies, stage plays, and operas.

BRENDAN FREELY was born in Princeton in 1959 and studied psychology at Yale University. His translations include *2 Girls* by Perihan Mağden, *The Gaze* by Elif Şafak, and *Like a Sword Wound* by Ahmet Altan.